* * * * *

To Maureen

my wife, closest companion and dearest friend

* * * * *

ALSO BY MICHAEL C. COX

* * * * *

NOVELS

Once Upon A Term

* * * * *

SHORT STORIES

Facts and Fantasies – Volume 1

Facts and Fantasies – Volume 2

Facts and Fantasies – Volume 4

Facts and Fantasies – Omnibus

* * * * *

Facts and Fantasies

Volume 3

Cognac – l'eau de vie

Michael C. Cox

Mimast Inc

Mimast Inc

* * * * *

This book is a work of fiction. Names, characters, businesses, organizations, places, events, and incidents either are the product of the author's imagination or are used fictitiously. Any resemblance to actual persons, living or dead, events or locales is entirely coincidental.

* * * * *

This paperback edition published in 2015 by Mimast Inc

Copyright © Mimast Inc 2015,

Canadian ISBN 978-1-987926-02-6

All enquiries regarding this electronic edition to:

Mimast Inc
Edmonton
Alberta T6R 2H9
Canada
email: mimast@telus.net

Acknowledgements

Firstly, I must acknowledge a debt to the teachers who taught English language and English literature in my first five years at a Grammar school in my home town of Bristol. In spite of their efforts and best intentions, by the time I was sixteen I had acquired a taste for reading but not for writing. To be fair to those teachers, I felt at the time that I had so much to read and so little to write about.

I must acknowledge two of those teachers: Alex Mair, a Scotsman no less, and A.B. Reynolds, a somewhat eccentric Englishman. The former opened my eyes to literature by telling me to read Great Expectations by Charles Dickens. The latter opened my eyes to language by telling me to read out loud the first sentence in an exercise on syntax error: "Do not kill your wife with work, let electricity do it."

Secondly, I must thank my dear friend, Leif G. Stolee. He has encouraged me to write about people and events that have enriched my life over the past few decades. Leif's enthusiastic response to my stories has kept me at my computer and out of mischief. And I must mention here, James Stolee. He tempered his brother's enthusiasm with many well deserved criticisms of my writings.

Lastly but certainly not least, I must thank my wife, Maureen. She has always been my dearest and closest friend. She has watched over my grammar, corrected my spelling and made many constructive suggestions. Without Maureen's love and support, I doubt that I could ever have written a single word.

* * * * *

Needless to say, any mistakes in grammar and spelling, and any errors in facts used fictitiously, are my fault entirely. Nobody else is to blame.

* * * * *

THE FOUR STORIES

* * * * *

Deception and a deadly switch 7

A gorilla in the cupboard 11

Water of life 61

What the eye does not see 69

* * * * *

Author's note

The first two stories combine factual episodes and figments of my imagination in varied proportions. I have tried accurately to reveal the facts underlying both stories but my memory is not what it was. I have also tried to conceal the identities of the people involved. If I failed in the latter and thereby upset any former colleagues, may I point out I never intended to embarrass and, more often than not, the law seems to benefit lawyers rather than litigants. The third story is purely auto-biographical and the fourth story purely fictional but set in a real location.

DECEPTION AND A DEADLY SWITCH

The truth underlying this story is the foolish unsecured loans that two colleagues and I made to a former colleague and his brother in 1991. The name of the school, the names of the two companies and the names of the characters, apart from my own, are fictitious. I definitely lost money. I believe I was deceived. I think it best not to comment further.

* * * * *

The two men shook hands and parted. I saw them as I happened to glance out of the window of my classroom, on the upper floor of the school, overlooking the car park. What, I wondered, was Cyril Rainsthorp doing shaking hands with a dubious former member of staff? Even with senior colleagues such as myself, our Head of Classics refused to shake hands in order to minimise the risk of contagion – one of his favourite words derived, as he never hesitated to declaim, from the Latin verbs *tangere*: to touch and *contingere*: to touch on all sides or pollute.

My thoughts were interrupted by the bell to end morning school. As I reached the foot of the staircase, Cyril came through the main door into the foyer. The cold wind had brought a pinkish colour to his sallow cheeks and made his white hair even more dishevelled than usual. We walked side-by-side down the corridor to the staff common room.

'I thought I saw A Simpleton in the car park just now getting into a new red Mercedes.'

'Sorry, I'm not with you, old boy,' replied Cyril, giving me a sideways squint.

'Anthony Simpleton. Unfortunate name for a schoolmaster. Left here about three years ago to set up his own computer business.'

'Oh, I didn't know his first name was Anthony,' said Cyril, unconvincingly.

'Tony! Most of us called him Tony.'

'Oh! I didn't really know him. What did he teach?' he asked, seemingly without interest.

'Physics and mathematics.'

'Ah! I see. Bit of a boffin then? Clever chap was he?'

'Tony always thought so. Probably still full of himself.'

'I'm surprised a clever chap like that hasn't changed his surname by deed poll.'

'He seemed to take a perverted delight in his name,' I said. 'Did you know his middle name is Simon?'

'A worthy name. Two of the Apostles were called Simon.'

'True. Unfortunately, some of our rather less worthy pupils favoured the association of Simon with the nursery rhyme: *Simple Simon met a pieman going to the fair…*' I said, tailing off, not knowing the rest.

'*Said Simple Simon to the pieman, Let me taste your ware,*' continued Cyril. '*Said the pieman to Simple Simon, Show me first your penny. Said Simple Simon to the pieman, Sir, I have not any.*'

'Bad enough that our wretched pupils nicknamed him Simple Simon,' I remarked, 'Do you recall how quick our colleagues were to draw attention to his initials when the draft timetable was posted on the notice board.'

'His initials? Oh, good gracious!' exclaimed Cyril as the penny dropped. 'ASS! But…'

'Indeed. Fortunately our beloved headmaster had them changed to TSS. The mind boggles at what the Upper Fifths might have made of ASS.

It was in 1983 that Tony Simpleton began his five-year teaching career at Lytchett Upper, our minor league independent boarding school for boys. During that period, Dr Trevelyan Wynne Evans, our fiery headmaster and former Welsh Rugby International, would from time to time ask me as chairman of the staff common room and Head of Science what I thought of Tony as a colleague and teacher. Trevelyan and I were a similar age and hoping to retire early. The staff saw us as the elderly bastions of the old school, being of one mind on the subject of *discipline* (masters were paid to teach and pupils were required to learn) and *uniforms* (blazers and badges for the boys; suits, ties and gowns for their masters).

Tony did wear a suit. It may have been a good fit once upon a time. We only ever saw the coat buttoned up at Sunday morning chapel. Tony's considerable bulk was a possible benefit when he was on the field in rugby kit but the bulge around his middle (courtesy of the ale he drank at the local village tavern) was an unequivocal deficit when he was straining his voice and the buttons of his suit in the staff pews.

Over the summer holiday between his first and second year at the school, Tony grew a thick beard. Staff opinion on it was divided. The geographers, grammarians and scientists said he grew it to compensate for his advancing alopecia. The classicists, historians and linguists said he wanted to hide his youthful features. A small minority which included myself and, I suspect, Dr Evans, believed he grew the beard to make it hard for us to tell if he was wearing a tie.

According to the few Oxford and Cambridge graduates on our staff, England has only two universities. Those of us who graduated from civic universities, such as Bristol, Exeter and Southampton were equally disdainful of the *New Polytechnics*. Tony emerged from a *Poly* somewhere in the Midlands and was offered a post at our school chiefly because he was the sole applicant but also because he claimed to share our headmaster's enthusiasm for rugby. He became a fairly competent teacher of mathematics, physics and rugby in spite of his antics much frowned upon by senior staff and, if truth be told, by the more intelligent of his pupils. Tony would prance around in his rolled-up shirt sleeves, perspire profusely and bellow at the pupils to get stuck in. Such a performance and such urgings may have been appropriate on the field but in the opinion of his heads of department there was no place for them in the classroom or the laboratory.

As far as one could tell, Tony had few if any friends on the staff. His principal enemies were the non-smokers who took great exception to the foul-smelling cigarettes of Turkish shag tobacco he rolled in a little machine and smoked in the corner of the common room. He did acquire a small following amongst the younger pupils when he formed a computing club which convened two evenings a week to write programmes and play games on the early machines such as Sinclair's ZX Spectrum, Commodore's Commodore 64 and Acorn's BBC Micro.

When the mathematics department introduced computing science into the curriculum, Tony was asked to teach it. When a computer room was set up for use by the mathematics and science departments, Tony was called upon to maintain it. When computers were introduced into the school office, Tony was asked to train the office staff and to service their machines. Tony became our computer expert. So nobody was surprised when, after five years as a perspiring teacher, he resigned his post to set himself up in business.

'How's his business doing these days?' I asked Cyril as we entered the common room.

'Rather well,' said Cyril. 'He's just formed a second company in point of fact.'

'Was that what you two were talking about in the car park?'

'Yes it was in point of fact,' said Cyril with a *mind your own business look.*

'Want you on his Board of Directors, does he?' I asked wryly.

'In point of fact,' retorted Cyril, catching sight of the slightly sardonic look on my face, 'he's looking for investors.'

'I see. He touched you for a loan.'

'Not at all. He's offered me a short term investment opportunity with a return of 13%.'

'Are you the first one he's approached?'

'In point of fact,' said Cyril, yet again uttering his favourite phrase, 'in point of fact yes, I am.'

'You're what?" asked Christopher Lovell, our Head of Music, who overheard.

'He's the first one that Tony Simpleton has touched for a loan,' I said.

'An investment,' snapped Cyril. 'He's asked me to invest in his new company.'

'Office Developments (International) Ltd? Is that the company?' Chris asked.

'Yes, I think that's the name,' replied Cyril.

'Then you're not the first. He's already asked me,' said Chris.

'How much does he want you to invest?' asked Cyril, somewhat crestfallen.

'Five thousand pounds. Is that what he asked you for?'

'Yes,' replied Cyril, 'with a return of thirteen percent.'

'If that's 13% per annum,' I said, 'perhaps I should put in £5,000. I'm only getting 7% on my building society savings.' In hindsight, what I should have said was *Thirteen percent sounds too good to be true; so what's the catch*? but I fell victim to the cardinal sins of envy and greed. Pride and wrath were to follow later.

* * * * *

We had no difficulty finding the place. A SIMPLETON'S COMPUTER SUPPLIES was printed in large letters high up on the long wall of the warehouse bordering the car park. The front entrance into the warehouse was equally easy to find, set as it was in the short wall and beneath the word ENTRANCE printed in the same large letters. The pair of thick metal security doors were wedged back to allow customers access to a carpeted foyer and a pair of glass doors.

A small, simple logo was frosted onto the glass of each door and a larger version, printed in black, dominated the centre of the foyer carpet.

A Simpleton's

Computer Supplies

Tony designed the logo himself and put it everywhere; on letterheads, supply notes and invoices, the stock, the goods and packaging, the employees' overalls and company sweaters, even the washroom towels; nothing except the toilet paper was spared.

Cyril led the way into the tiled reception area. Chris and I followed. A barren counter, facing the entrance and running the width of the area, was roughly divided into three unequal sections by the signs hanging from the ceiling above. Cyril ignored the RETAIL and the TRADE sections and led us to ENQUIRIES.

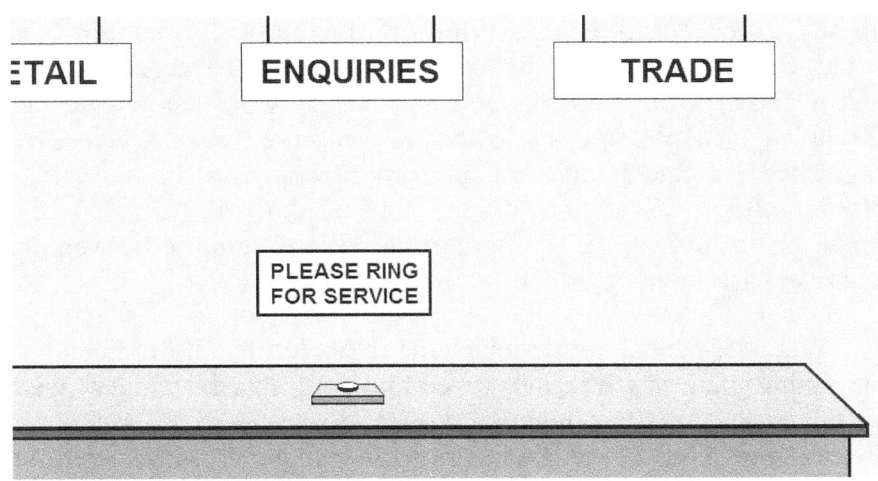

I braced myself for his invective against enquiries – it should be *inquiries*; *inquire, inquiry*, from the Latin *in* – in and *quaerere* – to seek – but his mind was elsewhere. Cyril was intending to put at risk, without his doughty wife's approval, a significant proportion of his retirement nest egg.

There was an open doorway in the wall behind the counter. Voices echoed through it but nobody appeared until Cyril, in response to the *notice please ring for service*, pressed the button on the counter. There was something familiar about the face of the young fellow who responded to the bell but I couldn't for the life of me think what it was.

'Good morning sir. What can I do for you?' he asked Cyril pleasantly with an accent suggesting he hailed from somewhere in the Midlands.

'These two gentlemen and I wish to see Anthony Simpleton.'

'Is he expecting you?'

'In point of fact, yes,' said Cyril, 'we have an appointment for 10 o'clock this morning.'

The young chap was solidly built and made the dark blue company sweater bulge in all the right places, giving a certain dignity to the quirky company logo on his chest. His auburn hair, neatly combed and parted down the middle, was starting to thin. He had a clear, healthy complexion and clean, white teeth which he displayed in a pleasant smile that he preserved even when Cyril suggested he change the notice from *please ring for service* to *please push for attention*. 'I am not,' said Cyril, 'a motor car requiring an oil change. Neither am I a bride wishing to be wed nor a corpse wishing to be buried.'

When he picked up the telephone in his left hand, I noticed that the young man was wearing a wedding ring, that his fingers were unstained and that his fingernails were clean and short. A thought crossed my mind as he spoke into the telephone with a definite Midlands accent, 'Tony! Mr. Rainsthorp, Mr. Lovell and Dr. Cox to see you. Will you come down or shall I bring them up?' After a short pause, he put down the phone, joined us on our side of the counter and said, 'Please follow me.'

He opened a door marked Private and led us up a wooden staircase to an uncarpeted corridor along which the four of us clattered until we reached a door whose upper half was panelled

14

with glass bearing the inevitable logo. Without knocking, the young man opened the door and led us into a sparsely furnished room. It was Simple Simon's office.

Tony hauled his bulk out of a large, plush-leather swivel chair and waddled from behind a large desk to greet us, his dark blue company sweater bulging in all the wrong places. He extended his podgy hand first to Cyril who was still wearing his soft leather driving gloves; the redoubtable Mrs Rainsthorp would no doubt sterilise them on his return home. As I gripped Tony's surprisingly limp, clammy hand with its nicotine-stained fingers, I recalled what scientific research had established; that one hundred different hands could yield more than 4,500 different species of bacteria and that one typical hand could be home to about 150 different species. A shiver went down my spine as I wondered what corrupting or harmful influence (or contagion as Cyril would say) Tony was spreading.

'Would you organise some coffee, Reggie,' Tony said as he waved us into three wooden foldaway seats arranged in a semicircle with their backs to a four-drawer metal filing cabinet. We took our somewhat uncomfortable places and waited. As Tony returned to his soft leather chair, I noticed that he had lost more hair in the three years since he had left our school; he was thinner on top and his beard was now quite neatly trimmed; it was too short to hide even the top of the polo-neck shirt he was wearing under his company V-neck sweater. When Tony was seated, I studied his desk.

Although the ashtray in the centre of the desk was empty and appeared unused, a smell of stale Turkish tobacco hung in the air and began to impregnate the clothing of we three non-smokers. The three trays (in, pending and out) at one end of the desk seemed as unused as the ashtray; in point of fact, as Cyril would say, they were empty but not necessarily unused. At the other end of the desk there was a bright red telephone and a polished granite pen holder. The ashtray and pen both bore the company logo.

Tony produced a box file, presumably from a drawer in his desk, like a magician pulling a rabbit from a hat, and flipped open the lid. I half expected a white dove to fly out. 'I've assembled some information about our new company and the product it will be

15

launching internationally,' he said, handing each of us a rather glossy brochure. 'Perhaps you'd like to look it over while we're waiting for the coffee.'

To my untrained eye the document Tony handed us looked quite professional. The pages were securely bound by a hard plastic spine. The glossy appearance was achieved by one clear plastic sheet atop the front cover which bore the company logo and the words *Offering Memorandum issued by Office Developments (International) Ltd*. The first few inside pages set out the details of this offering in what I supposed was a legal format. The narrow left-hand column bore short titles (The Issuer, Name, Head Office. The Offering, Securities offered, etc.) associated with the sections and individual paragraphs in the wide right-hand column.

On the first page, one paragraph in particular caught my eye. It occupied more than one third of the length of the wide column and consisted of just one sentence which was sprinkled with words such as debenture, heretofore, non-convertible, notwithstanding, redeemable, retractable and unsecured. The later pages included sections on financial statements and business plan details that were just as obscure. My head was still spinning when I came across the management biographies section. Just as I saw the photo of Reginald Stephenson alongside Anthony Simpleton's picture, Reggie walked into the room with the coffee.

* * * * *

'More coffee?'' asked Tony, addressing the three of us. We shook our heads. 'If you'll clear away the coffee cups, Reggie, I'll set up the overhead projector,' said Tony, as he conjured up the machine from behind his desk. While he was adjusting the focus of the company logo projected onto the wall we were facing, Tony informed us that his younger brother, Reggie, would explain the business side of the new company. When I turned to the two pictures in the biographies section of the *Offering Memorandum* and saw the brotherly resemblance, I asked Tony why his brother had changed his name to Stephenson.

'Reggie's second name is George. When he was a boy his hero was George Stephenson who invented the first steam locomotive to run on railway lines.' When Chris said it was called *The Rocket*, Tony immediately corrected him with, 'No! It was the *Blucher* in 1814. That was the first steam locomotive. George and his son Robert built *The Rocket* fifteen years later when they invented its multi-tubular boiler.'

Reggie returned and stood by the overhead projector, cutting short any further discourse on the topic of steam locomotives. He introduced himself as Tony's brother and outlined his intention to explain their offering memorandum, the structure of their new company and their business plan. We learned that Office Developments (International) Ltd was a private company owned jointly and solely by Tony and Reggie. Only the three of us – Tony's former colleagues – were being privileged with the opportunity to invest in their new company by purchasing a corporate bond; to *get in on the ground floor* and so share the company profits.

Their business plan was to build a network of independent distributors, starting with the UK and then extending overseas. When I asked Reggie what the company was going to distribute, Tony replied with, 'It's called *Ink-Up*. I'll tell you all about our product in a minute.' Reggie continued by displaying overhead transparencies of various projected sales charts and ended with a titillating table of anticipated profits to swell our retirement nest-eggs.

'What *exactly* is this corporate bond of yours?' asked Chris.

'It's actually a debenture,' said Reggie confidently.

'From the Latin phrase *debentur mihi* – there are due to me,' said Cyril, giving us the correct literal translation.

'So it's an I.O.U. and you are asking for a loan,' said Chris.

'The £5,000 debenture is a non-convertible, non-redeemable, non-transferable, unsecured, fixed term, fixed interest, *corporate bond*,' recited Reggie a little less confidently.

'In other words, a loan,' said Chris.

'Is the fixed term three years and the fixed interest thirteen percent?' I asked.

Tony nodded.

'Is that thirteen percent *per annum*?' I stressed the last two words.

Tony nodded again.

'So that means after three years you'll pay me back my five thousand pounds plus three times 13% of £5,000, correct?'

'That's a good point,' said Chris, nodding at me and then looking hard at Tony.

'When we repay your principal on the debenture's redemption date, we were thinking...' Tony tapped the keys of a calculator he had conjured from his desk drawer and mumbled, 'nought... point... one... three... times... five... nought... nought... nought...'

'Six hundred and fifty pounds?' I questioned rhetorically.

'Um, yes. £650. That's it,' said Tony.

'Per year that's about £217...,' I said, taking out my calculator. 'Actually two hundred and sixteen point six recurring... or four point three recurring per cent per annum,' I stated, having divided the 216.66666 by 5000. When I continued crisply with, 'My building society gives me 7% on my safe as houses, risk free savings account. So...' Tony hastily cut me off.

'No! Sorry. My mistake. It is 13% per annum, of course, and you would get...' He tapped his calculator keys again. 'You would get a return of £1950 on your principal.'

'I can't speak for Cyril and Michael,' said Chris, 'but I'd want the interest paid monthly.'

'So should I,' said Cyril.

'Same here,' I said. 'Could you pay it directly into my bank account?'

'Certainly,' said Tony without batting an eyelid. 'That can be arranged. Just give Reggie your bank account details and he'll do the rest. OK. If there are no more questions, it's my turn. I'm going to tell you about *Ink-Up*. It's a bit technical but I'll try not to blind you with science.' Tony then treated us to a lecture that was gratifyingly short and, I had to admit, most interesting.

The *gunsmiths* E. Remington & Sons produced the first Type Writer (as they called it) over 139 years ago in America; Christopher Scholes and Carlos Glidden invented it. They made and sold fewer than five thousand but they started something which was to lead to the modern typewriter and dot-matrix printer. Incidentally, they patented the QWERTY keyboard (now called the *universal keyboard* and used on all modern computers) which they designed to space apart the most widely used letters in order to minimise the clash (or sticking together) of a pair of typebars. Now even if Remington sold only 5000 Type Writers, they would have sold thousands more type writer ribbons.

Scholes made his ribbon from cotton. Later ribbons were made of silk. When the cotton and silk was needed in World War II, nylon was used but the ribbons were stiffer than the silk ribbons, held less ink and produced printing that was less sharp. Even silk ribbons do not last forever. The ink eventually runs out and we throw the ribbon away. Last year Western Europeans threw away more than 160 *million* ribbons – about twelve thousand tonnes in weight and worth about £600 *million*!

Ink developed in China more than five thousand years ago was a mixture of soot, oil and gelatine from animal skins. In the 15th century when Gutenberg turned a wine press into a printing press, an ink was developed (from soot, turpentine and walnut oil) that would stick to the paper but not blur the letters. Modern ink is a complex colloidal mixture whose ingredients are designed to control the viscosity of the liquid, the speed at which the ink dries and the appearance of the ink when it is dry.

'This is where *Ink-Up* comes in,' enthused Tony. 'I have scientifically developed and tested an ink that we can spray, from a non-pressurised environmentally-friendly canister, onto typewriter and printer ribbons so they can be used over and over again. The canister is made of aluminium and is recyclable. A canister of Ink-Up retailing at £12.95 will save the customer at least 90% of the cost of buying new ribbons.' Tony paused for breath and would, I suspect, have conjured up his Turkish cigarette making machine had he not been facing a trio of anti-smokers. 'Any questions?' When we shook our heads, Tony led us downstairs and through another doorway into the warehouse proper. Reggie followed along behind us.

The large area seemed half empty to me but probably half full to Tony. Occupying one half of the floor space were several long lines of tall metal shelving on which boxes of various sizes and colours were stacked. The other half of the floor space was empty save for a small rectangular building about 10 feet long and 6 feet wide. It was made of bricks and mortar. Its flat metal roof with its 6 inch metal lip seemed to be clamped down, onto the four brick walls, the way the metal lid clamped down on Tony's tobacco tin to provide an airtight seal. The brick shed – for that's what it really was – had a solid metal door in the short wall but there were no windows.

Tony flipped the two switches on the outside wall, explaining that he was putting on the extractor fan, in the small end wall, to remove any fumes that just might be inside, before putting on the fluorescent light that ran down the middle of ceiling. When Cyril asked why, Tony explained that the fumes and the air could form an explosive mixture that arcing in the light switch might detonate. *Arcing in the fluorescent light could also detonate explosive mixtures*, I thought to myself, especially since Tony didn't allow much time for the fumes to be extracted and since there seemed no way for fresh air to be drawn into the hut he called his *laboratory*.

After a few moments, Tony opened the door for us to look inside. Down the right-hand wall was a bench supporting odds and ends of scientific equipment (a balance, several measuring cylinders, and some funnels), various bottles, a machine that looked like an oversized kitchen blender and a few empty aluminium canisters. Down the left-hand wall were stacks of plain cardboard cartons

20

which, we were told, were packed with *Ink-Up* canisters ready for dispatch. When I asked Tony why his logo was not on the boxes, it was Reggie who answered me.

'*Ink-Up* is produced and distributed by ODI - Office Developments (International) Ltd, an entirely separate company from SCS - Simpleton's Computer Supplies.

'So you're saying the two companies have nothing to do with one another?'

'That's right,' said Reggie, 'they are separate legal entities/'

'But you and Tony own both companies, don't you?' I said.

'Yes, that's right,' said Tony, butting in, 'but the two companies are quite separate.

'Which company owns this brick hut?' I asked

'SCS.' Said Reggie. 'ODI just pays SCS a *nominal* rent to use it.'

The three of us left by the deliveries entrance and found ourselves in the car park close to Cyril's Ford Fiesta. It was raining so we dashed for the car. Once inside, we gave some thought to our encounter with Tony and Reggie. Cyril seemed to have the most doubts about parting with five thousand pounds. Chris pointed out that Tony was really asking for an unsecured loan but willing to pay a high interest for it.

I recalled that our Head of Economics, commenting upon the adage *low risk low gain, high risk high gain*, said that investments with a high return may be risky but investments with a low return need not be safe. With inflation running at 12%, a safe investment in the bricks and mortar of a building society deposit account yielding 7% would be losing value. Then I remembered my father used to say *a faint heart never won a fortune* when he went to post his football coupon; it was his version of the saying *a faint heart never won a fair lady*. When the three of us finally agreed we should lend Tony the money, I said rather prophetically, 'Nothing ventured, nothing gained.'

* * * * *

The school year of 1990-1991 was memorable for several reasons. Our robustly fit headmaster, Dr Wynne Evans, fiddled his retirement on the grounds of ill health and left at the end of the Michaelmas Term. The Second Master took temporary command and held the fort for the Hilary Term. On the basis that my salary as a senior master could pay for two young teachers able to coach sports, I persuaded the new headmaster to let me go. I did think it diplomatic to refer to my two possible replacements as *young* rather than *inexperienced*. So, I took early retirement at the end of the Trinity Term.

Chris Lovell, at least ten years my junior, also left that summer to become Head of Music in an International School somewhere in the Far East. Cyril Rainsthorp was destined to remain at the school for a while longer until his teaching career came to an abrupt end. At the beginning of the Summer holiday, Chris, Cyril and myself handed over our cheques to Reggie Stephenson and collected our £5000 debenture bonds.

On the 23rd of September 1991, a credit of £40.62 appeared on my bank account. It was from Office Developments (International) Ltd. I thought it should have been £54.17 until I remembered that ODI had to withhold £13.54 as a tax to be paid to the Inland Revenue. When I saw that £40.62 + £13.54 = £54.16 I realised that Tony and/or Reggie had rounded 54.16666 *down* to 54.16 and *not up* to 54.17 thereby robbing me of 1 penny. Then I chided myself for being niggardly. What was one penny out of 5,417 pennies? The money was rolling in.

A year passed. During that time I occasionally heard from Chris extolling the benefits of working in an American-run school, being paid in Hong Kong dollars, and teaching so many beautiful girls. With his keen musical ear he had little difficulty coping with the four tones of Cantonese and soon learned to speak the language; the reading and writing of Chinese was another matter altogether. The 56,000 or so complicated characters were bad enough but when they all occupy the same space and run together on a page so you have to work out where each word starts and finishes, well who but the Chinese would bother. Chris was on a five-year contract; he planned to return to England before the island's sovereignty transferred in 1997 to the People's Republic of China under the Sino-British Joint Agreement. He was rather blasé about his monthly credit from ODI.

Cyril, by contrast, was like a cat with the cream. I saw him at the school's 1991 Christmas concert to which I was an invited guest. 'How are you, old boy,' said Cyril, beaming broadly but taking care not to offer me his hand. 'Pleased with our monthly return on our corporate bond, are we?' At my cautious *so far so good response*, he tut-tutted and said, 'Still have reservations, do we?' I still felt it too good to be true but I simply asked Cyril what his wife thought about it. 'In point of fact,' he replied, 'I haven't mentioned it to Marjorie yet. No need you see.' I didn't see and I rather suspected that Cyril also feared the venture might be too good to be true.

In September 1992 on the anniversary of the first payment, the thirteenth deposit of £40.62 appeared on our accounts. October and November saw two more such credits. The money usually appeared in the first week of each month. On the 22nd of December, a damp and chilly Tuesday, I telephoned my bank.

'No, I'm sorry, sir, there's no mistake. The cheque received from Office Developments (International) Ltd was not honoured.'

'What do you mean,' I asked, 'not honoured?'

'It failed to clear.'

'What do you mean,' I said, 'It failed to clear?'

'There were no funds in the account to cover it.'

'In other words,' I gasped, 'it bounced.'

'I'm afraid so, sir. Merry Christmas!'

'Cyril here. Is that you old boy?' whispered the voice when I answered my telephone.

'Yes, Cyril, it is,' I said. 'How are you? Ready for Christmas?'

'Look here,' whispered Cyril, 'I thought I'd better ring you about ODI.'

'What about ODI?' I asked as if I couldn't guess.

'They haven't paid me this month's interest. Have they paid you?'

'Yes and No,' I said.

'What do you mean, yes and no?'

'My bank got the cheque as usual but it bounced.'

'Oh, no!' said Cyril loudly. Then more quietly and in a calmer voice to his wife, 'No Marjorie, sorry my dear. Nothing's wrong. I'm on the telephone. Be there in a minute.'

'Let's not panic, Cyril,' I said. 'Leave this with me. I'll find out what's going on.'

Chris Lovell said he was probably coming home to spend Christmas with his parents, so I rang their number. Mrs Lovell confirmed he was back for Christmas but said he had gone out to do some last minute shopping. I left her my number and made it clear that I wanted to speak to her son as soon as he came in.

'Hello Chris. Thanks for ringing.'

'Mother thought it sounded urgent. What's up?'

'Have you checked your bank account today?'

'I've just drawn heavily on it but otherwise no, I haven't checked it.'

'Do you know if you got your monthly payment from ODI?'

'Now you mention it, I didn't,' said Chris, not sounding concerned.

24

'Neither did I and neither did Cyril. The cheques bounced.'

'Oh dear. I'll bet our classicist is in a flap.'

'That's putting it mildly. Any chance you could come with me tomorrow to find out what Tony and Reggie have been up to?'

'Tomorrow? Wednesday? Yes why not.'

'Thanks. I'll pick you up in the morning. 10 o'clock OK?'

'10 o'clock is fine with me. See you then.'

I parked near the warehouse delivery entrance, next to a familiar Ford Fiesta, and we walked around the building to the front entrance. The security doors were wedged open as before. Through the glass doors we could see Reggie behind the TRADE section of the counter. He was smiling pleasantly to a tall white-haired fellow with his back to us. We entered and the glass door closed behind us. Reggie looked in our direction and asked, 'Have you come to see Tony?'

'Hello Cyril,' said Chris. 'Three minds with but a single thought.'

'I thought you were in Singapore,' said Cyril who seemed to have aged ten years since I had seen him just a few days before at the 1992 School Carol Service.

'Hong Kong, Cyril. Hong Kong,' said Chris.

'I don't think Tony is in yet,' said Reggie, reaching for the telephone.

'I should like to see for myself,' said Cyril heading towards the door marked private.

Reggie hurried from behind the counter and dashed ahead. When we entered the office, Tony was hurriedly trying to clear his desk of a mound of paperwork and what looked like account books. The ash-tray overflowed with cigarette ends and there was an unfamiliar sickly odour mingling with the smell of Turkish tobacco smoke in the hazy blue atmosphere.

On a small trolley alongside the leather chair was a computer whose monitor was displaying a complicated spreadsheet. Tony was red-faced and flustered. As he struggled to close an account book with his left hand and switch off the monitor with his right, he appeared to me like a second-rate magician unsuccessfully trying to perform a new trick. Cyril probably saw him as an overweight schoolboy whom he had caught red-handed in the act of some mischief.

'Sorry,' said Tony. 'I wasn't expecting you. I'm rather busy right now. Could...'

'I didn't get my cheque this month,' barked Cyril. 'I'd like to know why not.'

'Could you organise some coffee, Reggie,' said Tony regaining some composure.

'What's going on?' asked Reggie.

'Coffee, Reggie, there's a good chap,' said Tony.

'We haven't got any coffee. Sorry,' said Reggie apologetically to us, before turning to face his brother again. 'What's this about Mr Rainsthorp's cheque?'

'It's not just my cheque, young man,' said Cyril. 'It's all our cheques. They bounced!'

'They bounced?' said Reggie. 'I don't understand.'

'It's just a bit of a mix up. It's a cash-flow problem. I'm sorting it out now.'

'I wrote those cheques myself,' said Reggie. 'They shouldn't have bounced.'

'I don't care who wrote them,' said Cyril angrily. 'They bounced. I want to know why.'

'So do I,' said Reggie, glaring at Tony. 'What have you been up to?'

Sensing a family row brewing, Chris and I dragged a protesting Cyril out of the office, down the stairs and through the door into the warehouse. It was neither half full nor half empty; it was at least seven eighths empty. There was only one line of metal shelving and there were very few boxes on the shelves. The brick laboratory stood out like a tiny oasis on the concrete desert of the large warehouse floor. I guessed correctly the switch for the extractor fan then made my fellow creditors wait a few minutes before I switched on the light and opened the door. There were bottles and equipment on the bench and a stack of cardboard cartons against the left-hand wall much as before. We stepped inside.

The smell of paint thinners and other flammable liquids was almost overwhelming; so much for the efficiency of the extractor fan. I suspected that the door hadn't been opened in quite a while. I wondered what might have happened if I'd switched on the light first. One large bottle bore a label *Acetone – Highly Flammable* on which was a red diamond with a 3 in the middle, indicating on a scale from 0 to 4 a *serious fire hazard*. When I unscrewed the stopper, Cyril said, 'That smells like Marjorie's nail varnish remover.'

'That's just one of the minor uses of this stuff, Cyril.'

'Is it dangerous?'

'This large amount in this confined space is very dangerous. Acetone has a very low flash point; minus 20 centigrade.' Seeing the blank look on his face, I explained that a mixture of acetone vapour and air above minus 20 centigrade could explode. 'If memory serves me, as little as ten percent acetone in the air could blast this brick hut to rubble.'

'I don't much like the sound of that,' said Cyril. 'Marjorie has a bottle on her dressing table. I think I should…'

'I don't think there's much chance of Marjorie blowing up your house. You should be more worried about the toxic effects of acetone.'

'What do you mean, toxic effects?'

'If you inhale a large concentration of acetone vapour, it could damage your central nervous system and cause nausea, headaches and dizziness. You could become unconscious and fall into a coma.'

'I don't think I should like to get trapped in this hut with that stuff in the air,' said Chris who had just opened one of the thirty cardboard cartons. Then he changed the subject by saying, 'Look what's in this box, you chaps.'

The cardboard carton held two dozen full *Ink-Up* canisters. Based on its weight, we judged the other twenty-nine cartons also held two dozen full *Ink-Up* canisters. So, altogether we reckoned that there were 720 canisters for sale at £12.95 each.

'This lot is worth £9,324,' Chris said. 'That's £3,108 apiece if we each take 240 canisters and sell them for £12.95 a canister.'

'Don't forget we have already had £609.30 in interest,' I said. 'So £3,108 plus £609.30 equals...'

'What are you two babbling about,' interrupted Cyril. 'I'm an investor not a salesman. I want to know what they've done with my money.'

'Judging from Reggie's reaction to our news,' I said, 'I rather think the question is *What has Tony done with our money?*'

'He did seem pretty upset,' said Chris, stepping out into relatively fresh air of the warehouse. 'Let's come back tomorrow and have a word with him.'

'With Tony?' said Cyril.

'No, Cyril. With Reggie,' I said, closing the laboratory door and switching off the light and extractor fan.

'Let's speak to him now,' said Cyril, striding off towards the door behind the enquiries, retail and trade counter.'

* * * * *

Reggie was captain of soccer at his school and almost made the England National Under-17 team. At the age of eighteen he was given a trial by Wolverhampton Wanderers FC but he really wanted to be a mechanical engineer not a professional footballer playing for Wolves. He managed to get a place at Wolverhampton Poly on the strength of his modest A-level examination results but he eventually dropped out because he couldn't cope with the mathematics.

His clean-cut appearance and pleasant personality secured him several jobs which he failed to hold down. He was working as a sales assistant in a TV and electronics store when Tony persuaded him to join his private limited company Simpleton Computer Supplies. He soon learned what *private limited* and *join* meant; the company was limited to Tony, the sole director, and young Reggie had *joined* as an underpaid employee of his older brother.

When Tony was going to form Office Developments (International) Ltd, he persuaded Reggie to buy into the company – ten thousand shares at £1 per share – and become an equal partner. Reggie expressed concern at the cost but Tony had reassured him that he would get his money back in three years from dividends and his share of the profits. So Reggie gave Tony his savings and raised the rest with a bank loan. That was a couple of months before the three of us had parted with our money. So the question in the minds of the four of us was *What did Tony do with £25,000*?

'Can you get hold of the books?' I asked Reggie.

'The books?'

'The company accounts,' said Chris.

'Yes, I suppose so.'

'I saw a spreadsheet just now on the computer in Tony's office,' I said to Reggie. 'Can you get a backup of all the data files from that computer?'

'Yes, I suppose so,' he said again.

'Good. I'd like those books and files by tomorrow.'

'That's Christmas Eve,' said Reggie.

'Well spotted,' said Chris. 'Merry Christmas.'

Cyril Rainsthorp looked a ghastly colour by the time he reached his car. Although he assured me he was fine, I was worried about him, especially when I saw the way he drove out of the car park and I heard the squeal of brakes; he had pulled out without checking that the main road was clear. He was lucky; the driver of the oncoming vehicle applied his brakes in the nick of time.

Before I turned the key in the ignition to start my car, I asked Chris what he thought of the whole business. He didn't seem all that concerned about the possible loss of his £5,000 and twenty-one months interest at 13%. 'There's no gain without risk,' he said. 'Anyway, it's not over until the fat lady sings.' I wondered where that expression came from.

Chris was sure it had nothing to do with large females ending operas with an aria. 'It's a popular but unsupported theory,' said Chris. 'Not all operas end with a solo from the heroine and not all female opera singers are fat. It might stem from the popular saying *Church ain't over 'til the fat lady sings*; quite a few church choirs in the Southern States of America are falsely reputed to consist of generously proportioned females.' When I asked Chris what he thought was the origin of the saying, he replied, 'I like the Kate Smith theory. She was a very large woman who popularised Irving Berlin's song God Bless America and had her own late-night TV show. The station always closed down for the night immediately after her last song.'

The next day, in the afternoon of Christmas Eve, Reggie showed up at my house with various documents, account books and computer disks. After we had left the previous day, Tony apparently dodged all Reggie's questions. One thing led to another and they had a terrible argument that might have ended in blows if Tony had not stormed out of his office. 'That was the last I saw of him,' said Reggie. 'I closed up the building at 9 o'clock and went home. When he never appeared this morning, I grabbed all this stuff you said you wanted and here I am.'

'Are you any good with accounts and spreadsheets,' I asked Reggie.

'To be honest, I haven't a clue. Tony handled that side of the business.'

'But you wrote and signed the cheques, didn't you?'

'Yes, I did,' said Reggie sheepishly but that was all. 'I looked after the warehouse and dealt with the customers. I'm not really much good with figures but I get on well with people. Tony's the opposite. He's very good at mathematics and computing.'

'I know someone who'll help me make sense of these books and spreadsheets,' I said, thinking of Quentin Frobisher, my former colleague and Head of Economics.

'Can I hang on to all this for a while?'

'The warehouse is closed now until Monday the 4th January. My wife and I are going back to Wolverhampton for Christmas to see our parents. Tony's supposed to be coming too. We should all be back on Sunday the 3rd January. I usually open up the building in the morning, so I'll pop round here first thing Monday morning if that's alright with you.'

'That should be fine, Reggie. Thanks. If you're back early on the Sunday, give me a call. Perhaps you could come and see me then.'

* * * * *

My luck was in. Quentin was at home when I telephoned after Reggie had left. I told him that I had some accounts and needed his

31

help. I didn't go into details and I didn't bring up Chris or Cyril's name. Quentin Frobisher was, like myself, one of the old school who believed in uniforms for the boys and gowns for the staff. He was a formidable and highly respected teacher. Many of his pupils gained Open Scholarships to Oxford or Cambridge.

Quentin himself obtained a First at LSE (The London School of Economics and Political Science, to give it its full name). Before he entered the teaching profession at age forty, he trained, qualified and worked as an accountant for a prestigious firm in London; he eventually became a Fellow Of The Institute Of Chartered Accountants In England And Wales. He did not suffer fools gladly.

I believe that all his pupils would remember the first time he spoke to them. They would see standing in front of them a tall, slender gentleman, wearing a white shirt and bow tie with a matching silk handkerchief cascading from the top pocket of his dark grey, three-piece, pin-striped suit. They would see beneath his dark, furrowed eyebrows a pair of piercing blue eyes looking over the top of a pair of gold-rimmed, half-moon spectacles balanced on the end of a thin nose. They would see his hair precisely parted down the middle, brushed back from his forehead and matching in colour the steel grey of his neatly trimmed moustache. And they would hear him say, 'Good morning, gentlemen. You are about to embark upon a two-year journey of discovery in the complex and difficult world of Economics. I am here to teach. You are here to learn. It may reassure you to know that I shall expect from you neither more nor less than I expect from myself.'

I arrived at Quentin's house on Sunday, the 27th of December, at 10:30 in the morning and was welcomed inside to the aroma of freshly ground coffee.

'Black would be fine, thank you,' I said, knowing that my host frowned upon anyone spoiling the taste of coffee by adding milk or, God forbid, cream. 'Your wife…'

'Elouise has gone to church to pray for our souls.'

'You don't go?'

'Not during the holidays, except for midnight mass on Christmas Eve. The knees of my trousers get enough wear and tear every Sunday morning during school term.'

'I hope you don't mind my…'

'If I had minded, dear boy, I'd have said so when you telephoned last Thursday. So, what's the problem?'

'I think I've been had.'

My telephone rang on Tuesday morning at 9:30 a.m. at precisely the time Quentin said he would contact me. One hour later, Elouise opened the door and led me through the house to their sunny conservatory. As she poured me a cup of freshly ground Douwe Egbert's coffee, Quentin put aside his Times newspaper and looked at me over his half-moon glasses.

'You have been had, dear boy, and quite cleverly at that.' It came as no surprise but it still upset me to hear him say so. 'I see he's taken our resident classicist and our musical émigré for a ride as well.' I nodded. 'I shouldn't imagine Christopher will lose much sleep over it. £5000 will be pocket money compared to his salary and perks in Hong Kong.'

When I said that our former music teacher hadn't seemed all that bothered, Quentin said, 'You never can tell. None of us likes to be robbed and even the mildest mannered soul can turn nasty. There was a case in the paper recently of a 76-year old grandmother who put a young mugger into hospital when he tried to steal her handbag.' When I deplored the fact that the old lady had been charged with assault, Quentin punctiliously quoted Mr Bumble in *Oliver Twist* by Charles Dickens: *the law is a ass*. When I asked him how he thought Cyril might react to being robbed, he said, 'That, my dear boy, is a very good question.'

When we had finished our coffee, we retired to Quentin's study. There were two leather armchairs facing the fireplace. The wall on either side of the bay window was hidden from top to bottom by solid oak shelves filled with books; many were leather bound and many, I should guess, were first editions. Behind the door and against the wall opposite the fireplace was a wooden roll-top desk; on it's pulled out writing section were Tony's account books. Alongside the antique desk was a modern metal trolley holding a printer and computer whose monitor was displaying one of Tony's spreadsheets. Quentin sat in his swivel chair. I sat by him on a chair he had fetched from the dining room. Before he even uttered one word, I asked myself why I hadn't consulted him *before* I gave Tony my money. Experience teaches even fools; *experientia docet stultos* Cyril would have said.

'So we've been had?'

'I'm afraid so.'

'How?'

'Quite simple really,' said Quentin. 'You lent money to Office Developments Ltd which transferred your money to Simpleton Computers Ltd, a company heavily in debt.'

'But ODI and SCS are *separate* companies. How could that happen?'

'Ah, now that's the clever bit. Firstly, SCS raised ODI's rent.'

'But Reggie said...'

'Tony's naïve brother, Reginald Stephenson?'

'Yes. He said that ODI just pays SCS a *nominal* rent for that brick laboratory.'

'I should hardly call £12000 per annum *nominal*.

'A thousand pounds a month. Why the...'

'Secondly, SCS charged ODI £250 per annum for lighting and heating and £400 per annum for cleaning.'

'Cleaning! What cleaning? You could plant seeds in the dust on the lab bench.'

'Thirdly, ODI paid SCS £12000 per annum in management charges.'

'Management charges?'

'ODI hired its staff from SCS.'

'What staff?' I asked but I knew the answer before Quentin replied.

'Anthony Simpleton and Reginald Stephenson, of course,' said Quentin.

'But… But…' I stuttered, 'Those two were joint sole owners and directors of ODI. How can they charge themselves for hiring themselves to themselves. It doesn't make sense!'

'Ah but you see, dear boy,' said Quentin. '*They* were not doing the hiring and charging. Their companies were. And they and their companies are separate legal entities.'

'What else did their *companies* do?'

'They paid their directors salaries, of course,' said Quentin.

'Salaries?'

'SCS paid Mr Anthony Simpleton, its only director, £1250 per month.'

'What about Reggie?' I asked. 'What did SCS pay him?'

'Very little I expect. He was an employee of SCS, not a director. Mr Stephenson is, however, an equal partner in ODI, the company which owes you money, but if these accounts are anything to go by, I believe your friend Reggie is worse off than you.'

'Why do you say that?'

'He and his brother are equal partners and directors of Office Developments (International) Ltd so they are equally responsible for its debts. Unlike Simpleton Computer Supplies Ltd, ODI did not, as far as I can tell, pay its directors a salary or any dividends on their shares. So, your friend Reggie has not been paid for his work and he stands to lose the £10,000 he paid for his shares which, being private shares, he cannot sell and which look to become worthless.'

'The rotten crook.. We'll have the law on him.'

'Unfortunately, dear boy, Mr Anthony Simpleton has not done anything illegal. So PC Plod will not be tapping his truncheon on Anthony's head let alone his front door.'

'We'll sue him then.'

'Waste of time,' said Quentin in his matter of fact voice. 'He's broke and being the crafty scoundrel his surname belies, he will no doubt shortly file for bankruptcy.'

'Poor old Reggie,' I said, beginning to feel genuinely sorry for him.

'He may not be that poor,' said Quentin. 'It looks as though both companies had directors share protection and life insurance in place.'

'What does that mean?'

'If a director/partner were to die, share protection insurance provides cash for the company to buy the shares of the deceased from their beneficiaries. In the case of Office Developments (International) Ltd, if Mr Simpleton were to die then Mr Stephenson would, for all practical purposes, collect on the insurance.'

'How much might that be?' I asked.

'£100,000.'

'One hundred thousand pounds! I wonder if Reggie realises this?'

'You might ask him the next time you see him, dear boy. Anyway, Let me take you through these accounts.'

For the next hour Quentin showed me how to read company accounts and distinguish between a profit & loss statement and a balance sheet. He explained that both basically deal with *assets* (what a company owns) and *liabilities* (what a company owes) but the P&L covers a period of time (3, 6 or 12 months) and the balance sheet gives the financial position on a given day.

As we looked through Tony's accounts Quentin bandied terms such as fixed and current assets, net asset value, EBITDA (earnings before interest, tax depreciation and amortisation) and operating profit. He was in danger of losing me when he introduced *liquidity ratio* (current assets divided by current liabilities) and calculated the value for Simpleton Computers. When I asked somewhat naively what it meant, he said, 'Anything less than 1.0 is bad news. This value of 0.006 is extremely bad news.'

* * * * *

'One hundred thousand pounds? Are you sure?' gasped Reggie.

'No, Reggie, I'm not sure but it should be easy enough for you to check. Look for the policy document. It's probably somewhere in Tony's filing cabinet.'

'So according to your friend, we've been had?'

'Good and proper, Reggie, and there's nothing we can do about it.'

'I'm not so sure about that,' he replied giving me a strange look as I got up to answer the front door bell.

'Chris! Cyril! Come on in. Reggie's already here. Find yourselves seats. I'll be with you in a tick.' As I returned with a tray of coffee and biscuits, I heard Cyril's raised voice.

'That brother of yours has robbed me of my savings. He's a crook and should be in gaol.'

'Careful, Cyril, that's slander.' I said as I handed out the coffee. 'Quentin assured me that Tony has done nothing illegal.'

'We should sue the scoundrel,' said Cyril, lowering his voice a little.

'Waste of time. According to Quentin, Tony's broke and will probably declare himself bankrupt.'

'We cannot just do *nothing*. We can't let him get away with our money,' fumed Cyril.

'What do you suggest?' said Chris. 'Turn him upside down and shake the coins out of his pockets?'

'I don't think any money would fall out,' said Reggie, 'but the contents of his tobacco tin might be of interest to the police.'

'Look here,' said Cyril, 'I don't want the fellow locked up on a drugs charge. I just want my money back.'

After we had all felt suitably sorry for ourselves, that meeting on the 3rd of January 1993 broke up. Cyril left first in a huff and drove down the road even more erratically than before. He worried me. In spite of our advice and what he had heard, he was determined to have it out with Tony. As I gathered up the coffee cups I heard Reggie asking Chris if he knew anything about electrical wiring. 'A bit,' said Chris.

He was being unduly modest. Chris knew a lot. He completely rewired the stage sound and lighting; he saved Lytchett Upper a small fortune. When I returned from the kitchen, I heard Chris say, 'Tomorrow morning then. Eight o'clock at the warehouse. I'll bring a couple of screwdrivers. We shouldn't need anything else if it's just a couple of wall switches you want looked at.'

After lunch I sat down and read my Sunday newspaper. The sorry state of the world and the desperate plight of others helped to put my relatively small financial loss into perspective. Quentin had pointed out that the £5000 wasn't a complete write off. I had received £609.30 in interest payments and I could set the £4390.70 loss against my capital gains. Even though I had no capital gains, I appreciated Quentin's trying to cheer me up. I put all thoughts of

Tony's skulduggery out of my mind and settled down to the Telegraph crossword.

Monday the 4th of January 1993 came and went quickly. Although I was only in my second year of retirement, I was already routinely wondering where the days went and how time flies; tempus fugit as Cyril would probably say in his retirement; a state he was not destined to achieve. I cannot remember what I did that day but I recalled that Chris was to see Reggie in the early morning and to catch his 12-hour flight out of Heathrow in the late afternoon. It was just after breakfast on Tuesday the 5th of January when I answered the telephone and heard Marjorie Rainsthorp's voice.

'Marjorie! *Marjorie*. Calm down. I can't understand what you're saying.'

'It's Cyril,' she sobbed. 'There's been a terrible accident. He's dead.'

'Dead? Are you sure?'

'Yes. The police have just been here. They looked the same age as my own children. The young woman police constable… Oh dear! Was that right? Are they still WPCs? She was very sweet…'

'*Marjorie*! Tell me what happened? Was any other vehicle involved?'

'Vehicle? What do you mean, *vehicle*?' said Marjorie. 'I don't understand?'

'It was a traffic accident involving his car, wasn't it?'

'No. It was nothing to do with his car. I know he's been a bit… not reckless exactly. No, not reckless. Careless perhaps. He's had a lot on his mind lately but he wouldn't tell me what was bothering him. Do you know what it was? He said he came to see you last Sunday… I thought perhaps…'

'Marjorie,' I said in a firm, quiet voice, 'how did Cyril die?'

'The policeman said he was...' she started to sob, 'they said he'd been killed.'

...and our political correspondent reported the rumour that in the forthcoming budget, the Prime Minister, Mr John Major, intends to replace the controversial Community Charge, a Poll Tax introduced under Margaret Thatcher in 1990, by a Council Tax.

Turning to local news... An explosion occurred today in a warehouse on an industrial estate. At least one person is believed dead. Nearby buildings are undamaged. Police and the fire brigade are on the scene. The cause of the explosion is as yet unknown.

Now over to the weather centre for the latest forecast.

It was several days before a more detailed report appeared in the newspaper and I read that the explosion had occurred inside the A SIMPLETON'S COMPUTER SUPPLIES warehouse and that the bodies of two men had been identified, that of Cyril Rainsthorp, Senior Classics Master at Lytchett Upper and... 'Two policemen to see you, dear,' said my wife, showing the uniformed men into my study.

'Good morning, sir,' said the inspector. 'My name is Trustcott. This is Sergeant Preston.'

'We're conducting inquiries into the explosion at a local warehouse. You may be able to help us. Do you mind if my sergeant takes notes?'

'No, not at all, inspector,' I said shaking my head. 'How can I help?'

'I understand that you knew the gentlemen who died in the explosion.'

'Yes, I did,' I said. 'They were colleagues.'

'Can we start with Mr Rainsthorp? How well did you know him?'

'Well, he and I were heads of departments at the same school for over ten years…'

'That would be Lytchett Upper?' said the sergeant.

'Yes, that's right. He was Head of Classics and I was Head of Science.'

'You are a chemist, is that right Dr Cox?'

'Yes. My Ph.D. was in Physical Chemistry.'

'I understand,' said the inspector. 'My son's doing chemistry at Bristol. He hopes to do a Ph.D. in Organic chemistry. Anyway, getting back to Mr Rainsthorp. I gather from Mrs Rainsthorp that her husband came to see you last Sunday. Is that right?'

'Yes.'

'How did Mr Rainsthorp seem to you?'

'How do you mean?' I asked.

'Did he seem upset? Was anything bothering him, would you say?'

'Cyril was… Look, I don't believe he told his wife this… He was in a flap because he had just discovered that he had, in his words, been swindled out of money he'd put aside for his retirement. When he left here he was extremely agitated.'

'Have you any idea how much money, sir?'

'A little over five thousand pounds,' I said thinking of the twenty-one months of interest we wouldn't get as well as the £4390.70 loss we could set against capital gains.

'Can you think of any reason why Mr Rainsthorp would be at that warehouse at the time of the explosion?'

'He could have been looking for Tony Simpleton.'

'Ah, yes. Mr Anthony Simpleton, the owner of the warehouse. You knew him I believe.'

'Yes. He taught for five years at Lytchett Upper before leaving teaching to start his own business.'

'And Mr Rainsthorp thought that Mr Simpleton had swindled him?'

'Yes.'

'And why should he have thought that, sir?'

At this point it seemed easier to explain how Tony had borrowed Cyril's money and used it to pay off some of his debts. When the inspector asked if I had visited the warehouse, I said that I had. When he asked why, I explained the reasons. When the sergeant asked if I had seen the brick hut and been inside it, I nodded.

'We think it was some kind of laboratory. Would you agree, sir?'

'That is what Tony, sorry Mr Simpleton, called it, inspector.'

'Could you tell us what was in it?'

'A bench with bits of equipment on top and various bottles of liquids underneath. That was on one side. There were cardboard boxes stacked on the other side. They contained aluminium canisters of ink for spraying on printer and typewriter ribbons.'

'Were these canisters pressurised?'

'Not in the usual sense of *pressurised*,' I said, 'but the ink contained volatile liquids and the canisters were capped. So...'

'They might explode under certain circumstances?'

'Yes. They might very well,' I said.

'What about the liquids in the bottles under the bench; do you know what they were?'

'I think they were the volatile liquids Mr Simpleton used to make his special ink.'

'Dangerous, were they sir?'

'Yes, sergeant. One or two were highly flammable and therefore very dangerous.'

'One last question, sir,' said the inspector. 'In your professional opinion, how safe do you think the laboratory was?'

'Let me put it this way,' I said, 'any decent Health & Safety inspector would have closed him down like a shot.'

As soon as the two policemen had left, my first thought was to call Chris in Hong Kong but then I remembered we were eight hours behind in Britain and realised my fellow creditor would be asleep in bed. I telephoned the next day; he was out. It was five o'clock in his afternoon when I tried again on Sunday the 10th of January.

I was just in time. He was getting ready to go out, to a restaurant and then to a *Music for Christmas and New Year* concert, at St. John's Cathedral, with the Hong Kong Chamber Orchestra conducted by Jerome Hoberman. 'Pity you're not here,' said Chris. 'They're doing The Christmas Oratorio by Bach; Handel's Messiah: A Sacred Oratorio, Part 1 and the Hallelujah Chorus from Part 2, …'

'Sorry to cut you short, Chris, but I've some terrible news. It's about Cyril Rainsthorp.'

'What about Cyril?'

'He's dead.'

'We've all got to go sometime, old chap. Heart attack was it?'

'No. He was killed.'

'Car crash?'

'No. An explosion in Tony Simpleton's warehouse.'

'You still there Chris?'

'Yes, I'm still here,' he said after what musicians call a *lunga pausa*. 'When did it happen?'

'Early last Tuesday morning.'

'Any idea how it happened?' Chris asked in what seemed a nervous voice.

'The police are investigating. They were here on Friday asking me what I knew about that brick hut Tony called his laboratory.'

'What did you tell them?'

'I told them what was inside the hut and that it did not comply with the Health & Safety at Work Act,' I replied. 'I should simply have told them it was a death trap.'

'Poor old Cyril. What a way to go,' said Chris in a strange voice.

'It was quick, I believe, and he didn't die alone,' I said. 'The police identified the bodies of two men at the scene.'

'Who was the other... Was it Reggie?'

'Why do you think the other man was Reggie?'

'I just thought... Didn't Reggie say he was always first there, to open up the warehouse early in the morning.'

'Yes, he did. In point of fact,' I said, thinking of Cyril, 'it was Tony.'

Perhaps I was mistaken but I thought I heard Chris utter a sigh of relief, especially when I told him that I thought the police were treating the deaths as accidental. At the mention of Reggie, I realised that I had not seen or heard from him for a week; curiously, the police hadn't asked me if I knew him. 'Look, I don't want you to be late for your concert but may I ask what you and Reggie were talking about last Sunday?'

'I don't rightly remember?' Chris replied unconvincingly.

'Sounded to me like he was picking your brains. Something to do with electrical wiring?'

'Oh, yes. That's right. He wanted my help to fix a switch.'

'Not the two switches on the outside wall of that brick hut, by any chance?'

'As a matter, it was. He wanted me to check the wiring. Something about the extractor fan not always coming on. He thought the switch might be faulty.'

'Was it?'

'No. It looked OK to me. We checked the wiring in the light switch while we were at it.'

'Reggie watched you dismantle those switches and put them back together again?'

'Yes he did. He seemed very keen to learn. I was surprised that he had never in his life wired a switch and didn't know how to shut off the power at the fuse box. Come to think of it, he didn't even know where to find the mains switch.'

'That's what he led you to believe anyway,' I said. 'Very interesting. I'd better let you go. You'll be late for your meal. I assume you're not dining alone.'

'No, not alone. I shall be enjoying the company of a colleague; charming young lady who is, as Eddie Duchin wrote *Lovely to look at, delightful to know*.' As he rang off, I had a vague recollection that the line continued with *and heaven to kiss*; but I could be wrong.

* * * * *

45

It was the 1st of April. I remember because I was skimming an article in the paper about a legal action, brought in the European Community, against British Gypsum Ltd and BPB Industries plc who were, according to their accusers, the Commission of European Communities, supported by the Kingdom of Spain and Iberian Trading (UK) Limited, monopolising the supply of plaster and plasterboard in contravention of Article 86 of the EEC Treaty governing competition. Just as I was coming to the conclusion that the article was not an April Fools Day joke, the front door bell rang. It was Reggie Stephenson.

'I'm sorry not to have been in touch,' he said. 'The past three months have been rather hectic as you can imagine.' I hung up his tailored overcoat and waved him into a chair. He looked the picture of health sitting there in his smart corduroy two-piece suit. His polo-neck shirt was woven from a fine, cream-coloured wool – pure cashmere I believe – that was not blemished by a logo of any kind. His socks and shoes matched the rest of his outfit in colour, style and, no doubt, expense.

After my wife had brought in the coffee and closed the study door behind her, Reggie said, 'I really did mean to get in touch sooner but what with one thing and another.' I sipped my coffee and waited for him to continue. 'How did Mrs Rainsthorp take her husband's death?' I lifted my shoulders, tilted my head and took another sip of coffee. 'It's all my fault you know. He should never have died like that. It was my fault... all my fault.'

According to Reggie, his brother came in very early on that Tuesday to work on the books. Cyril arrived shortly afterwards and brushed past Reggie who was wedging open the metal security doors. He heard Cyril shout at Tony. When Reggie looked round, he saw his brother dodging behind the counter and Cyril following him. Reggie was in the car park by his car when he heard the explosion. He ran back to the front entrance to find the foyer carpet covered in shards of glass. An acrid smoke was billowing through the open doorway behind the counter. He put a handkerchief over his nose and mouth and managed to dial the emergency services from the telephone at the enquiries end of the counter. The worst moment was when they brought out the two badly burned bodies.

'Why do you think Cyril's death was your fault, Reggie?' I asked quietly.

'I shouldn't have let him in. I could see he was in no state to tackle Tony.'

'What do you think caused the explosion?'

'All I can think is that Tony dashed to his laboratory to get away. Mr Rainsthorp ran after him. In the rush Tony probably didn't give the extractor fan enough time to work.'

'Or perhaps he switched on the light first,' I said.

'Oh, he wouldn't have done that. Tony knew which switch was which and he was always careful to put on the fan first. Mind you, it had been playing up. I asked Mr Lovell to take a look at the switches for me but he said the wiring was fine.'

'The police recorded the deaths as accidental, I believe.'

'Yes. They did. They were very thorough. They asked me a lot of questions about the stuff in the laboratory that I couldn't answer. I hope you didn't mind but I said that you might be able to help.'

'I told them what I could, Reggie. I think they were satisfied.' As I said that, a terrible question came into my head. Did I screw the stopper back on that bottle of acetone?'

As Reggie was leaving, he shook my right hand and placed an envelope in my left. When his red Mercedes was out of sight, I returned to my study to find my wife gathering up the coffee cups. 'He seemed a nice young man,' she said. 'Wholesome. Yes, wholesome.' When I picked up my souvenir of Paris letter opener, my wife said, 'What have you got there?' I slit open the envelope and handed it to my wife. 'Goodness me!' she exclaimed.

My first phone call was to Hong Kong. Chris had just finished his evening meal. 'What's that, old boy? Speak up. It's not a very good line.' He listened carefully to my question then said, 'Hang on a minute, I haven't actually seen today's post.' I heard the sound of an envelope being torn open and then a loud whistle. 'Hello! You still there, old boy?' When he knew I was still listening, he said, 'What a stroke of luck. Did you get one as well?'

My second telephone call was to Cyril's widow. 'Hello! Marjorie Rainsthorp speaking,'

'Hello Marjorie,' I said. 'How are you? Bearing up?'

'I'm as well as can be expected.' She was obviously still missing Cyril.

'Marjorie, did a smartly dressed young chap drop in to see you today?'

'In point of fact, yes. He said he was a friend of Cyril. I'd never seen him before.'

'No, you probably wouldn't have done. He was just somebody Cyril and I knew. He was really just a casual acquaintance.'

'It was odd, you see. He didn't tell me his name and he wouldn't come in. He just handed me an envelope and said it was what Cyril would have wanted me to have. I couldn't believe my eyes. Is it genuine? I mean it is April Fools Day.'

'I'm sure it's quite genuine, Marjorie. It's not every day somebody gives us cheques for ten thousand pounds.'

* * * * *

Epilogue

Two colleagues and I were foolish enough to lend a former colleague £5000 each. We did receive interest for fifteen months and we did set our net loss against capital gains; but we still lost more than £4000. At the time of writing, only one of my two colleagues is still alive; the other died of natural causes. I did teach for five years in an independent school but I was never Head of Science or chairman of a staff common room. There was a brick shed, located in a warehouse and subject to various charges. There was also a product for re-inking typewriter and printer ribbons but it was not called Ink-Up.

There were, I confess, moments when I should have liked to do away with the rogue who relieved us of our money but deep down I knew that if I were to commit such a crime and I were able to evade the law, I should not escape the judgement of my own conscience and the inevitable punishment it would inflict upon me for taking the life of another.

The London School of Economics and Political Science is a specialist single-faculty constituent college of London University and the only one of its kind in England. The LSE, located in Westminster and near the Courts of Justice and Temple Bar, is a world leader in research and the teaching of social science. It probably has the most international student body of any university in the world today.

The are several clichés in sports such as baseball, basketball, football and hockey that imply one cannot be sure of the result until the final whistle. Not all invoke a fat lady singing. Their origins are variously attributed to Ralph Carpenter, Dan Cook, Bill Morgan and Yogi Bera. Kate Smith, who helped to popularise Irving Berlin's God Bless America by singing it at the start of many hockey games, was fat. She once weighed 235 pounds.

Acetone is used as nail varnish remover and the hazards mentioned in the story are true. It is very volatile and its vapour does form an explosive mixture with air, the percentages ranging from 2.5 to 12.8 by volume of vapour; a static discharge could detonate it. Acetone should never be stored in a refrigerator with an interior light switch.

49

A GORILLA IN THE CUPBOARD

This story concerns a real event I witnessed and a likely consequence I imagined. I have not named the school where this occurred or used the real names of the teachers and pupil concerned in order, hopefully, to avoid costly legal actions. To any former colleagues who were also witness to the event and who might think themselves unfavourably portrayed in my story, may I assert that the names and characters are the product of my imagination and any resemblance to actual persons, living or dead, is entirely coincidental.

* * * * *

During the time when I was a pupil and subsequently a teacher in England, the school year of about 38 weeks was divided into three terms by the Christmas, the Easter and the Summer holidays. Each term - winter, spring and summer - was usually split into two by a one-week break at approximately mid-term. To anyone who has never taught classes of up to 30 or so pupils at a time, teachers might seem to have a cushy life. Indeed, I had a friend who took great delight in asking me when I was going to get a proper job. He worked for a commercial company, 8-hours a day, 5 days a week, with a 3-week summer holiday and just a few days at Christmas, New Year and Easter.

I shall not attempt to argue a detailed case for teachers here. Suffice it to say, my salary was much lower than my friend's salary, I received no Christmas bonus or overtime pay, and I took work home evenings and weekends. Anyway, the point I wish to make is that my colleagues and I worked hard and were always glad when the last day of the summer term arrived.

'Settle down. The final bell hasn't gone yet. Make sure you clear everything out of your desks. Anything left behind may – I say *may* – end up in lost property. Problem?'

'Are you going on the French trip this summer, sir?

'Peut-être. Je ne suis pas certain. Desk lids open, gentlemen.'

'Sir, could I ...' The rest of his sentence was drowned by the loud final bell and the even louder noise of thirty boys banging down their desks lids and hurrying to the door.

When the last of my charges had disappeared, it took me a few moments to adjust to l'état de calme. It was almost twenty past two. Enough time for me to sort and file away various papers, tidy the books on my shelf and clear the top of my desk before the cleaners started their rounds. It was ten minutes to three when I walked into the staff common room to check my pigeon hole for any last minute memo from the Second Master and to scan the notice board. The invitation was still pinned up.

The High Master is pleased to invite all teaching staff to join him for sherry at 3 p.m.

As I entered the study, I was offered the statutory small glass of Jerez de la Fronteira 'Fino'. I prefer their 'Oloroso' but in the headmaster's opinion, nobody with a decent palate would countenance such a tipple. At precisely 3 o'clock, we were all present and as correct as we'd ever be. On the first chime of the clock in the college tower, Dr Anthony Saint-John Howard (pronounced 'sinjun' in the best circles) and his acolyte, the Second Master, entered. They circulated separately - the pair were nothing if not discrete - to exchange a few pleasantries.

'Looking forward to the French trip are we?' I was, as it happens, but the question was rhetorical. The good doctor had moved on before I could raise a faint smile. At 3:15 p.m. precisely, we turned to face the large, antique desk - in old oak to match the panelled study walls and bookcases - for the annual speech of thanks and congratulations for our jobs well done. At 3:30 p.m. precisely, we raised our glasses and drained the few remaining drops of sherry in support of the Second Master's reply on our behalf. The formalities over, we trooped back to the common room to start our long summer holiday.

'Listen up, chaps,' said Alan 'Jock' Crawford, 'we've organised a 100-yards staff dash for a bit of fun. We're starting at 4 o'clock.'

'I'm game,' said one of the new young members of staff. 'On the track near the 1st XI cricket pavilion?'

'*Gaudeamus igitur iuvenes dum sumus*!' quoted the Head of Classics. 'Therefore let us rejoice while we are young!'

'Come on,' said Jock, 'it's handicap race. The older you are the bigger the handicap.'

'Sorry, old boy, but my body is already my biggest handicap. I shall be happy to join the spectators. If I may quote Horace, '*Eheu fugaces labuntur anni.*'

'Alas, the fleeting years do slip by,' said Jock who taught Latin and ran the 1st XI cricket.

'Count me out,' I said, pulling a face, 'I've got a doctor's note for my arthritis.'

After some repartee from the master i/c rugby and a rather more erudite comment from the Head of History, Jock said, 'It's for fun. No running kit or running shoes allowed. We'll fire the starting gun at 4 o'clock sharp. Don't be late.'

That's how it started. A half-dozen took part. A few of us cheered them on from the pavilion steps. The rest of the staff went home. The following summer a few more took part. One of the runners wore a floppy sun hat. Another had a red bandanna around his forehead. A few more stayed behind to watch. One of the housemasters brought some cans of beer. At the end of the race, most of us stood around chatting for a while. Before we knew it, the summer end-of-term staff dash had become the excuse for us to gather and unwind over a bottle of beer or a glass of wine.

We'd put money in a kitty to cover the drinks and to buy the hamburgers which the Head of business studies would turn into burnt offerings on the barbeque. Some participants transformed the race into a costume parade. Straw hats. Coloured braces (suspenders in America) holding up baggy trousers. Bowler hat and umbrella. T-shirt from the Canary Islands. Even a pair of striped pyjamas. It was, after all, just a bit of fun. Clearly, however, with each successive year, the members of that merry band of runners were trying to outdo one another. Just when we thought the limit of this absurd competition had been reached, one of the least likely of our colleagues surprised us all.

* * * * *

It has been my lot to have taught boys only. It has been my further my lot to have taught in schools and colleges with highly qualified staff and extremely intelligent pupils. It has also been my experience to have encountered more than my fair share of eccentricity amongst both the staff and the boys.

In the five or six years leading up to what I shall call, with apologies to William Shakespeare, the summer of our content, the Head of music was fortunate in having an extremely gifted young pianist as a pupil. Indeed, this boy's solos in the school concerts were a delight. Moreover, his sensitive playing – always from memory – was of such a high standard that a senior colleague, who reported on the concerts for the school magazine, always wrote as though he were the Times music critic analysing the performance of a celebrated professional.

Now according to my tutees, it was well known to everybody except the Head of Music that this young pianistic prodigy was in the habit of borrowing a large number of long-playing classical records for the summer holiday. My sources told me that he would raid the music cupboard when the final bell had rung and the Head of music had gone to the common room. On the first day back - at the start of the winter term – I was assured he would return the records to the cupboard, sneaking into the music department early before anyone was about. In all previous summers, his visits to the cupboard had been uneventful. This time there was a surprise in store – in the music store to be precise.

* * * * *

The final bell had sounded. My papers were filed away. The books on my shelf were in ordnung. My desk was clear. The High Master's invitation was on the common room notice board as usual. His speech was as dry as his 'Fino'. His second-in-command's reply was as sweet as a Jerez 'Dulce'. The staff dash was all set for 4 o'clock. There was plenty of time to complete a few last minute chores in the common room. On my way there I thought I heard two noises. The first sounded like a grunt and the second like a scream. Both seemed to come from the music room. I probably should have investigated but I was suffering from end-of-year fatigue and just couldn't be bothered.

The department appeared to be deserted when Jeremy Fitzgibbon, our young pianist entered. As he approached the door of the large music cupboard, he was playing loudly in his head the piano part of *L'Éléphant mouvement* no. 5 - for double-bass and piano - from the musical suite *Le Carnaval des Animaux* by Camille Saint-Saëns.

The French composer's *groupe zoologique* had lions, hens, roosters, asses, tortoises, elephants, kangaroos, cuckoos, an aquarium, an aviary, a swan and even fossils. Ironically, it had no primates in any shape or form. Jeremy was still playing the waltz-like triplet figure on the piano and hearing the double-bass humming the melody - all in his head - when he reached the cupboard.

When he opened the door and stepped inside, his thoughts were on the records he would borrow. From within the darkness there was a muffled grunt. Jeremy switched on the light and screamed – out loud – and not in his head.

* * * * *

It was one of those hot, dry days with which the summer holidays rarely began. The aroma from the BBQ was already filling the air. The spectators assembled on the pavilion steps near the finish line. The gaily bedecked competitors were assembling at their handicapped positions in the distance. The starting pistol was raised.

'On your marks!'

'Get set!'

Before the gun could be fired, a gorilla lumbered into view and posed on the start line.

'I say, chaps, there's a gorilla on the track,' exclaimed a biology teacher.

'That's no way to speak of... crikey! You're right,' said one of the chemists.

'*Fallaces sunt rerum species*, as Seneca would have said,' quoted the Head of Classics. 'Old Seneca was right,' I thought, 'the appearances of things are deceptive. Who is that in a gorilla outfit?'

'*Vestis virum reddit,*' said our classics scholar, quoting Quintilianus.

'*Clothes maketh the man* is hardly appropriate, old boy,' said Jock. 'It's a gorilla suit.'

A mathematician started to tick names off a staff list to identify the gorilla by the method of elimination. The Head of History and former guards officer who ran the school cadet corps raised his pistol for a second time.

'On your marks!' he barked.

'Get set!'

The shot he fired into the air made the gorilla jump and take off.

'It's our music master! It's Tudor Williams!' exclaimed the Head of Mathematics. 'No one else on the staff has such uncoordinated legs. And the way his arms are moving, I'd say he's still conducting the school orchestra.'

All eyes were on the gorilla. He was going to be last but clearly not least. He was stealing the show. As he got closer to the finish line, his legs seemed to become progressively more uncoordinated. His last few yards to the line was a sight to behold. His arms and legs thrashed wildly and independently in different directions. He reached the finish line and then, to everyone's surprise, he staggered onwards for ten more yards and then collapsed.

It was a wonderful performance. He came in last but in a grand style unsurpassed to this day. We were all laughing and cheering even when he was on his back, all his limbs still thrashing wildly. Then Howard, the Head of Biology, grabbed me and said, 'Something's wrong.'

'We've got to take his head off,' said Howard.

'Shall I fetch a saw from the workshops?'

'This is no time for flippancy. He's in trouble. Help me with this zip.'

'What the ...?'

'He's hyperventilating. Help me get him into the pavilion.'

When we removed the head of the gorilla we recognised the face of Tudor Williams but only just. He might have been an astronaut in a rocket accelerating out of the earth's atmosphere, except that he was in a gorilla costume lying on his back on the school running track. His skin was waxy and grey in colour. It was stretched so tightly against his high cheek bones that it looked translucent. His cheeks were rippling and pulsating. His mouth was held open in a grimace. His lips were rapidly vibrating and noisily sucking in great gulps of air. I helped Howard lift him to his feet and heave him into the pavilion where, to everyone's relief, he recovered quite quickly.

'What were you thinking of?' we asked.

'I saw this outfit in the window of our local costume and fancy dress shop. I thought it would be a bit of fun.'

'It was fun until you fell over and we realised you were in difficulties.'

'Looks like I made a bit of a fool of myself, didn't I?'

'Nemo risum prebuit, qui ex se coepit,' said our elderly classicist quoting Seneca again.

'I beg your pardon,' said Tudor.

'Roughly translated,' said Jock, 'nobody is laughed at, who laughs at himself.'

'Fancy a hamburger?' asked Howard.

'Just give me a few more minutes and time to get out of this outfit. I'm boiling in it.'

'Fine!' said Jock. 'See you at the barbeque.'

'Tudor, old chap,' I said, 'when did you put on this costume?'

'Straight after the final bell.'

'Where did you put it on? Here in the pavilion?'

'Oh, no. I didn't want to be seen until the race was about to start. That would have spoilt the surprise.'

'So where did you put it on?

'In my music cupboard.'

'Did you hide in the cupboard till 4 o'clock?'

'Yes. It's the perfect place. Nobody goes there after the bell, do they?'

'No,' I thought, 'and young Fitzgibbon certainly won't be going there again in a hurry.'

* * * * *

Epilogue

There was a music master who put on a gorilla costume and hid in his music cupboard. There was a pupil who was in the habit of borrowing LP recordings from that cupboard for the summer holidays. It is, therefore, highly probable that the pupil encountered a gorilla in the cupboard.

There was a staff dash after school on the last day of the summer term. The music master did run in a gorilla costume on a hot, dry day and hyperventilate. And his appearance was much as I described. I did assist the Head of Biology that day but I taught Chemistry, not French.

For the record, hyperventilation (sometimes called overbreathing) is rapid, deep breathing leading to low levels of carbon dioxide in the blood. It is often caused by anxiety or panic. The overbreathing may exacerbate the anxiety and lead to a vicious circle of panic and hyperventilation.

WATER OF LIFE

The Bristol-Bordeaux family-to-family exchange began in 1947 with one teacher and twenty-seven pupils from Fairfield Grammar School. The scheme rapidly expanded. In the Easter of 1951, more schools – my own included – were involved and more than one hundred pupils took part - myself included – even though I was no longer studying French. In April 2007, the exchange scheme celebrated its 60th year jubilee.

* * * * *

In July 1950, we all sat at desks in the school gymnasium of Merrywood Grammar School For Boys to take what we called *the school cert*. It was the culmination of our five years of study. One incident stands out in my mind. As Roger and I entered the gym for the three-hour chemistry paper, I wished him good luck. My friend grinned and said he would leave as soon as the supervisor would let him.

Roger hated chemistry as much as I loved it. My best subject was his worst. From my seat near the back, I could see Roger at his desk near the front and on the far side of the gym. Whenever I happened to glance in his direction, he was writing and, to my surprise, he was still writing when the supervisor told us to put down our pens.

As soon as we were outside the gym I rushed over to Roger eager to know which six of the ten questions he'd tackled.

'Didn't do any,' he said.

'But you were writing for the whole three hours, weren't you?'

'No, not really,' he replied.

'But I saw you.'

'I wasn't writing,' he said with a grin. I wasn't answering any of those chemistry questions, if that's what you think,' he said with an even bigger grin on his face.

'So what were you doing if you weren't writing?'

'I was using the exam paper to play book cricket!'

Our exam results, which included a distinction in French for each of us, persuaded the school to admit us into the Sixth Form and persuaded our parents to bear the financial burden that entailed. In September 1950, Roger began the two-year Advanced Level course in French and, I believe, in English and Latin. I took chemistry, physics and mathematics. During that first winter term, James G Clark, the master i/c the Sixth Form and the language teacher, suggested it might be good for us to go on the Bristol-Bordeaux Exchange.

Mr. Clark – a Scotsman better known to us by his nickname 'Angus' – had tried to persuade me to do French and Latin, claiming they were my best subjects. I resisted by saying that I could learn languages in my own time but not chemistry and physics which required a laboratory for the practical work. Whether or not French was my best subject, I had enjoyed it and I was delighted when my parents let me go with Roger on the exchange.

For the last few weeks of the winter term and for all the weeks leading up to Easter, 1951, I could not rid myself of a very bad cold. I always walked to and from school with Roger and other friends. The school was at the top of a hill and reached by more than a hundred steps. When I arrived at the top I would be wheezing and coughing fit to die.

I felt bad. The fact that my face was covered in blackheads and boils made me feel worse. Our family doctor, Dr John Pollard, a delightful, elderly Irishman with a hearing aid as defective as the ear it was supposed to help, tried a range of medicines on me without success. The acne and acne vulgaris even resisted his three-week course of *arsenic*!

The infection on my chest and/or lungs may, or may not, have been bronchitis or pneumonia – *tis a mystery to be sure it is, that's what it is, a mystery* - but whatever it was, I still had it when the time came to depart for Bordeaux. Throughout the journey by train and cross-channel boat, I stifled my wheezing and coughing in a handkerchief and buried my ugly face in Dr Phillip Frank's biography of Albert Einstein. Roger, by contrast, in the pink of condition, dilly-dallied from Bristol to Bordeaux with young ladies from a variety of schools.

* * * * *

Our first unforgettable smell and taste of France was at a Youth Hostel in Paris. It was at breakfast (*le petit déjeuner*) - *l'arôme et le goût du café et des baguettes*. We drank the coffee from a large bowl. The bread was fresh from la boulangerie. Long and thin, crusty on the outside and soft inside, it was still warm enough to melt *du beurre* but not to affect *la confiture d'orange*.

That coffee, bread and marmalade was the best I have ever tasted. Although I have been back to France and to Paris (but not that hostel) since then, I have never managed to recapture the magic of that first breakfast. We were probably shown la *Tour Eiffel, l'Arc de Triomphe, le Sacré Cœur* and Napoleon's tomb at *les Invalides*. I have long forgotten. But I can still smell that coffee and taste that bread and marmalade.

The train journey from Paris to Bordeaux took most of the day. I had probably finished Einstein: His Life and Times by the time we arrived. Roger had probably filled his pocket notebook with names, addresses and telephone numbers. As soon as we were out of the train and assembled, we were introduced to our French *correspondants*.

'Bonjour. Je m'appelle Michael.'

'Bonjour. Je m'appelle Louis.'

My *correspondant* was two years younger and a few centimetres shorter than myself. His hair was dark and very curly. I envied the clear, sun-tanned skin on his face which, to judge from the dark fuzz on his upper lip and around his chin, had not yet felt the touch of a razor blade. He had been adopted by Madame Escary and lived with her at 146 Avenue de la Libération *au banlieue*, which I discovered meant in a suburb (called *le Bouscat*) on the outskirts of the town. We went there by tram.

En route, I practised my French and discovered that Louis spoke little or no English. Mme. Escary greeted me warmly in French – no English there either – but spared me the traditional embrace and kisses on the cheeks. My wretched skin and hacking cough had something to do with that I suspect.

'Tu veux manger quelque chose?' she asked.

'Non, merci Madame,' I replied with the best pronunciation my hacking cough would allow. 'Je n'ai pas faim.' I was tired not hungry.

'Mon Dieu! Tu est malade, n'est-ce pas?' she said.

I nodded. I was sick. I was sick of this hacking cough and infection for which Dr Pollard had found no cure. She disappeared into another room and returned to the kitchen, where Louis and I were sitting, carrying a large tumbler full of a pungent, golden brown liquid.

'Bois!' she said, handing me the glass. I took a sip. It had a horrible taste.

'Allez! Bois tout!'

I did as I was told and drank the lot. Some of Dr Pollard's remedies had been worse.

'Tu est fatigué, oui?'

'Oui, Madame,' I said honestly. It had been a long journey and I was ready for bed.

Louis led me outside the bungalow and into a kind of outhouse where I was to sleep. I do not remember much about it. On reflection, I think it may have been a wooden summerhouse. What I do remember vividly was the bed. At home I had a small, single bed. The kapok-filled mattress was thin and firm. I slept between cotton sheets under a blanket. This French bed was large. The mattress was very thick and filled with feathers. On top was *le duvet* - equally thick and also filled with feathers. I changed into my pyjamas and crawled under *le duvet* and onto *le matelas*.

* * * * *

When I woke up after what turned out to be 12-hours of sleep, I just could not believe it. I had slept on my back and I had not moved. I was no longer coughing and wheezing. I was delighted. As I started to get up, I found that my pyjamas, the mattress and the duvet were saturated with my perspiration. I was less delighted by that discovery. How would I explain this and apologise to Mme Escary? French in a classroom in England amongst English-speaking schoolboys and French in a home in France amongst French-speaking people proved to be two different languages.

'Bonjour, Madame. Bonjour Louis.'

'Bonjour, Michel. Ca va? Tu as bien dormi?'

'Oui, merci, Madame.'

Yes, thank you, madam. It was a totally inadequate response to 'How are you?' and 'Slept well?' But my mind was elsewhere. I may have perspired away litres of water in the night but I still needed to go to the lavatory. At my first attempt (*Oú est le cabinet?*) to ask where it was, Louis showed me a large cupboard filled with coats hanging on hooks. At my second attempt (*Oú est la salle de bain?*) he showed me a room with a bath and shower but no toilet. At my third attempt (Oú est la toilette?) we were back to the cupboard again.

All subsequent attempts led to this large cupboard. Finally, Louis took me inside and pointed to a hole in the ground in the corner. That was my first - but not my last - encounter with *des sanitaires français*. I do not remember what form of sanitation was in that Paris hostel. Whatever it was - or whatever they were (the term in modern usage - *les toilettes* - is plural) – it would not have been an elaborate toilet roll holder cum musical box from Switzerland. When I pulled off my first piece of tissue paper, the holder played Franz Lehár's Merry Widow Waltz!

At the breakfast table I managed to explain and apologise for the damp bed. *Ca ne fait rien*! I was glad it did not matter but I was embarrassed all the same. Then I endeavoured to discover what the medicine was that she had given me to drink.

'Excusez-moi, Madame. Qu'est-ce que c'était ce médecin que vous m'avez donné hier soir?' Louis was grinning from ear to ear.

'Quel médecin?' she asked.

66

She was justifiably puzzled. I had asked her what was *that doctor* you gave me yesterday evening! So, I tried again substituting that *medical science* (*cette médecine*) for that doctor. Finally, I got it right.

'Qu'est-ce que c'était ce médicament que vous m'avez donné?'

'Médicament? Ce n'était pas de médicament,' she said with a laugh and went to fetch the bottle.

'If it wasn't medicine,' I thought, 'then what was it?'

She returned and handed me a large bottle, saying, 'C'est l'eau de vie.'

I translated this literally - the water of life. Then I looked at the label on the bottle. I had consumed a tumbler full of Cognac Brandy!

* * * * *

Epilogue

Sometime in the summer term of 1951, 'Angus' told Roger he was not working hard enough and should choose between his studies and his piano playing. He chose. He closed his desk, walked calmly out of the classroom and never came back. He became a very successful professional pianist, conductor, arranger and composer. At the time of writing, details of his life and work can be found online. Sadly it fails to mention that my friend died some time ago. J. G.(Angus) Clark collapsed and died many years ago on supervision duty in the school playground.

Our school cert was the last of the First School Certificate Examinations. The following year it became the General Certificate of Education (GCE). Today it's the General Certificate of Secondary Education (GCSE). I shall not debate here the relative merits and standards of the education that I received as a schoolboy for those five years and that I delivered as a chemistry teacher for thirty years. I shall simply say that I relished those five years of schooling that prepared me for the last school cert. I still have my old 1950 examination papers. They challenged me then. I confess they challenge me even more now.

WHAT THE EYE DOES NOT SEE

My wife and I once owned some timeshare at Castillo Beach Club, a resort on the lower slope of a hill overlooking Caleta de Fuste on Fuerteventura in the Canary Islands. The reception, bar and restaurant were in the main area known as Lake. The other area, known as Moon, was on the other side of the Calle de Virgen de Guadalupe. There are still squirrels on Chipmunk Hill. The supermarket (El Supermercado) and restaurant (El Papagayo) may still operate. I am not sure. The characters and events in this story are pure fantasy but the settings are real enough.

* * * * *

'Good afternoon ladies and gentleman. We shall shortly begin our descent into Fuerteventura. At this time we ask you to return to your seats and fasten your seatbelts. Please place any hand-luggage in the overhead lockers or under the seat in front of you. All electronic devices must be switched off, tables should be stowed and seatbacks should be in the upright position.'

The Boeing 737 had taken 4 hours and 15 minutes to fly from a cold, damp England to a hot, dry island off the west coast of Africa, a distance, as the crow flies, of 1,719 miles from London Heathrow to Aeropuerto de Fuerteventura. Its passengers were mostly British. They would find no crows on the island and, for that matter, few other birds but they would find plenty of cats roaming wild. Only twitchers and cat lovers amongst these holiday makers would be interested. Their main concern was to tan their white bodies to the leathery brown of a well-worn horse saddle unaware, in all probability, of the pros and cons of sunbathing. Over-exposure to sunlight increases the risk of skin cancer. Under-exposure increases the risk of vitamin-D deficiency, leading to rickets in children and less resistance to skin cancer in adults.

'Where's my bottle of water, Florrie?'

'In your bag, Ernie. Under the seat in front of you by your big feet.'

'How did it get there?' asked Ernest.

'I put it there when you were keeping everybody awake with your snoring,' said Florence.

'Since when do I snore? You're a fine one to talk, you are ...'

'Oh shut up. We're landing in about twenty minutes. D'you want a boiled sweet?'

'No thanks. I'll pinch my nose and blow hard to unblock my ears,' said Ernest.

'The pilot said it was thirty-two degrees, clear skies and sunny in Fuerteventura.'

'What about the wind? I'll bet it'll be windy. It has been windy for the last five years,' snorted Ernest.

'He said nothing about the wind. You'd better have your hat handy. Keep the sun off that bald head of yours. I don't want you burnt on our first day, same as last year.'

The cabin crew made their final rounds. They collected earphones and newspapers. They held open black plastic bags for garbage. They checked that all seatbelts were fastened, that all seats were in the upright position and that all luggage was properly stowed in the overhead lockers or under the seats.

'Janet! ... Janet! ... Wake up, dear.'

'What ...? Oh goodness! I hope I wasn't snoring, Geoffrey?'

'We're starting our descent. Put your seat upright. I've stowed your table.'.

'How long was I asleep?' Janet asked.

'Most of the flight,' said her husband.

'Four hours? Did I really sleep for four hours?'

'No, probably not. More like three I suppose. Anyway, you needed the rest.'

'I was tired and these business class seats with their extra tilt... *so* comfortable,' said Janet stifling a yawn.

'Hear that? Sounded like the landing gear. We'll soon be on the ground,' said Geoffrey.

'What's the weather going to be like?' Janet asked.

'The pilot said it's very warm and sunny so everybody'll be wearing sunglasses.'

'I'm so glad we're going to Castillo Beach Club again, Geoffrey, I really am.'

71

Geoffrey Walters couldn't remember the last time he travelled economy class. He was tall and his long legs needed the extra space. And he could afford to pay the five times as much for his seats that Florence Broadbent had paid for her economy class seats. He, Geoffrey J. Walters, was after all a successful business man with an unwavering faith in the old Yorkshire adage *where there's muck there's brass*.

Geoff (as he was known to his Yorkshire parents) left school at sixteen and was apprenticed to a local plumber. One day they were called out to unblock a drain. It was in fact a sewer. The wily old plumber stood well back smoking a cigarette while the young plumber's mate, Geoff, tackled the job and became more than just wet behind the ears. That evening as he soaked in a hot bath and his father burnt his overalls at the bottom of the garden, Geoff recalled his encounter with that sewer.

To cut a long history short, Geoffrey J Walters completed his apprenticeship, worked hard, saved his money, bought his own van and specialised in clearing drains and sewers. Before he and his parents knew it, *Fast Drain Clear Ltd* had grown into a major franchise across Yorkshire, Lancashire and other parts of the North of England. G.J., as he was known to the members of the company who worked closely under him, became rich.

'That's the undercarriage opening, Florrie.'

'What?'

'I said that's the wheels coming down. Didn't you hear?'

'No I didn't, not above all the other noise going on. At least *your* ears are unblocked and your hearing's not impaired,' said Florence.

'No, I'm not *deaf* if that's what you mean. Got to be grateful for small mercies. Ears like a bat ... and *no*, they're not big and sticking out, thank you,' said Ernest.

'You said it, Ernie Broadbent, I didn't.'

'No, but the way you've been acting lately, I wouldn't put it past you, Florrie Broadbent.'

'We've not landed yet, have we?' Florence asked.

'Course not! Open your eyes and look out the window.'

'You're right. Silly me. We're still in the clouds. I hate landing.'

'And you hate taking off. Just relax and stop worrying,' said Ernest.

'Easier said than done. I'm not like you. I'll be alright once we're on the ground.'

'I hope so. You've been on edge ever since we left the house. Is it me?'

'No, Ernie, it's not you. I've just had a lot on my mind recently,' said Florence.

* * * * *

'Good afternoon ladies and gentlemen. Welcome to sunny Fuerteventura in the Canary Islands. The outside temperature is thirty-three degrees. Please remain in your seats with your seatbelts fastened until the plane comes to a complete stop and Captain Jackson switches off the seatbelt sign. Take care when opening the overhead lockers in case any luggage has shifted during the flight. Would anyone needing assistance please remain seated until the other passengers have deplaned. On behalf of Captain Jackson and the rest of the crew may I thank you for choosing Zipjet Airlines. We wish you a pleasant holiday and look forward to serving you again.'

'What was that you said Ernie?'

'I said what's wrong with disembark or just get off? Deplane! Another Americanism! What with spelling aluminium *aluminum* and sulphur *sulfur* I don't know where it's all going to end.'

'Oh for goodness sake stop moaning. We'll be getting off in a minute,' snapped Florence.

'There, you see. You said *getting off*. You didn't say deplaning!'

'Everything alright Mrs. Broadbent?' asked Melanie, one of the cabin crew – Ernest disliked the term *cabin crew* and preferred to call them stewards and stewardesses.

'Yes thank you,' said Florence.

'Do either of you need any help?' Melanie asked.

'No thank you, Melanie, we can manage. We're just waiting for everybody else to get off. Not much point in standing up. We'll have a bit of a wait for our luggage, won't we?'

'Very sensible,' agreed Melanie. 'I can never understand why everybody stands up before we open the doors or why they're in such a rush to get off.'

'Could you get my wife's bag down for her, Melanie?' said Ernest smiling ingratiatingly and making a mental note that Florence and the stewardess had said *get off*.

'No problem,' said Melanie. 'Which one is it?'

'It's the tartan wheel along case,' said Florence.

'Here you are Mrs Broadbent.'

'Thank you, Melanie,' Florence said. 'Come on Ernie, it's time for us to *deplane*.'

Fuerteventura airport at El Matorral was opened in 1969 for flights between the Canary Islands and European destinations. As the tourist trade grew, so did the airport. It now has an extended runway to cater for long-range aircraft annually ferrying more than four million passengers to the island.

The airport boasts a variety of shops, places to eat, an observation deck and a children's play area. It does not boast about the delays through passport control and customs or of the long waits at the luggage carousels now all too prevalent at international airports. And *El Aeropuerto* does not accept any responsibility for the lethargic taxi and shuttle services outside the terminal, let alone boast of them.

'Taxi, Señor?'

'Si! Quisieramos ir al Castillo Beach Club, por favor.'

'What was that you said, Geoffrey?'

'I said we should like to go to Castillo Beach Club, please,' said Geoffrey without a trace of his boyhood Yorkshire accent.

'Would you ask the driver his name?' said Janet.

'Cómo se llama Usted?'

'I am Alejandro Carlos Ramirez, Señor! Señora!'

'Do you speak English?' Janet asked.

'Yes. I learn at school. Do you speak Spanish, Señora?'

'No, I'm sorry, I don't but my husband does.'

'You learn at school, Señor?'

'Si! Clase nocturna,' replied Geoffrey rather casually.

'I too go evening class. You have good accent, Señor.'

'Gracias!' said Geoffrey deigning not to comment on Alejandro's English pronunciation.

Florence and Ernest Broadbent were last off the plane, last through passport control, last through customs and last to collect their luggage. When they joined the end of a rather long queue for a taxi, Ernest was considerably hot and not inconsiderably bothered. Florence was doing her best to remain calm.

'Taxi! Taxi!' yelled Ernest in his blunt Yorkshire accent.

'He heard you the first time, Ernie. Keep your hat on your head. Stop waving it about.'

'Buenas tardes, Señor! Señora!' said the driver smiling at Ernest and then Florence.

'Do you speak English?' Ernest asked unnecessarily loudly and in the worst tradition of the Englishman who assumes Europeans are deaf if they don't understand him.

'Si, Señor! I speak English.'

'Yo hablo español pero mi marido no habla español, Señor!' said Florence.

'What did you say?' Ernest asked his wife.

'I told him I speak Spanish but my husband doesn't.'

'Your wife speak Spanish very good, Señor. Where you are going?'

'Castillo Beach Club, por favor,' answered Florence.

'Very nice place, Señora. First time?'

'No, we have been before. ... Do you want to sit in the front, Ernie?'

'No. I'll get in the back and hold on to my flight bag. You can get in the front and practise the lingo.'

The airport was about three miles from Puerto del Rosario, the capital of Fuerteventura, and just five miles from the resort where Ernest and Florence would spend their week's holiday *if* they survived the taxi ride. Florence put on her seat belt and made sure Ernest did up his. The driver only ever bothered with his seat belt when *la policia* were around. He drove with his left arm hanging casually out of the window and the thumb of his right hand hooked loosely onto the bottom of the steering wheel. When he took his dark brown eyes off the road to look at Florence, she wished she hadn't asked him a question.

'Cómo se llama?'

'My name is Esteban, Señora. What is your name?' said the driver.

'Mi nombre es Florence Broadbent,' she said. And then she turned to Ernest and said,' Our driver's name is Esteban. Isn't that interesting?'

'I heard! What's so interesting about Esteban?' asked Ernest.

'Esteban is Spanish for Stephen. It's our son's name in Spanish,' she said to Ernest. Then turning to look at the driver, she said, 'Stephen es mi hijo. Stephen – inglés. Esteban – español.'

'Ah, I understand. Now I call myself Stephen. Is good?' said Esteban.

'Muy bien, Esteban. Mi hijo prefiere Steve.'

'Did you tell him to call himself Steve?' asked Ernest. 'What's wrong with Stephen?'

'No!' said Florence. 'I told him our Stephen prefers to be called Steve.'

'Mi marido se llama Ernest pero prefiera Ernie.'

'Ha-ha! Is funny, Señora Broadbent,' said Esteban.

'What did you say to him this time, Florrie?'

'I told him your name is Ernest but you prefer Ernie.'

'So? What's funny about that? What's wrong with Ernie?'

'Nothing. It's just that... well, why can't our Stephen be Steve if you can be Ernie?'

'We arrive, Señor y Señora. Castillo Beach Club! I bring your luggage.'

'Gracias, Esteban. ... Adios!' said Florence, paying the fare and including a nice tip.

* * * * *

The glazed terracotta tiles of the steps and path leading down from the road shone in the bright sunlight and would have been dangerously slippery if, in the extremely unlikely event, rain should fall on them. The red of the tiles contrasted sharply with the thick white walls of the building but not with the purples and reds of the thorny bougainvilleas bordering the entrance to *La Recepción*.

'Hola!' said Ana Maria, the pretty dark haired, dark eyed *recepcionista*.

'Buenas tardes, Señorita. Mi apellido es Walters,' Geoffrey said fluently.

'Buenas tardes, Señor Walters.'

'Hable inglés, por favor. Mi esposa no habla español,' said Geoffrey

'Of course. I'm sorry, Señora Walters,' Ana Maria said to Janet. 'I didn't realise you do not speak Spanish like your husband.'

'That's quite alright. I like to hear Geoffrey speaking Spanish,' said Janet.

'Please may I see your passports, Mr Walters?' When she had checked the passports, she handed them back to Geoffrey and said, 'Gracias Señor.'

'Which apartment are we in?' asked Janet.

'You are in apartment 46, Señora Walters,' Ana Maria said. Then she turned to Andrés, a tall, muscular sun-tanned fellow with blond hair and blue eyes who probably descended from the Guanches – the original natives of the Canary Islands. 'Las maletas, por favor. Apartamento cuarenta seis.'

'Gracias, Señorita,' said Geoffrey

'De nada, Señor. Here are your keys and TV remote. Please follow Andrew.'

Esteban, their dark-haired, dark-skinned, thick-set taxi driver, hurried ahead with their suitcases while Ernest held onto his wife's arm and used his stick to help him negotiate the tiled steps and path from the road down to the entrance and reception. Once inside the building, Florence wanted her husband to sit down but he refused. He stood alongside her while she spoke to the young lady behind the desk.

'Hola!' said Ana Maria.

'D'you speak English?' asked Ernest curtly before Florence could speak.

'Yes, of course, Señor. Good afternoon. Welcome to Castillo Beach Club. Your name is?

'Broadbent. Dr. and Mrs. Broadbent. We were here last year. Don't you remember?'

'Ah, si! Señor y Señora Broadbent. No, sorry. I am new here,' Ana Maria replied.

'Ah! I thought I didn't recognise your voice. What's your name?

'Ana Maria, Señor.'

'What a lovely name. If I'd had a daughter I might have called her Anne Marie,' said Florence before Ernest could say any more. 'Here are our passports.'

'Thank you, Señora.'

'What's our bungalow number then, lass?' Ernest asked.

'Your apartment is number 47, Señor.'

'And where's that exactly? Lake or Moon?'

'It is here on Lake, Señor,' said Ana Maria, smiling at Florence.

I hope it's not next to that noisy bar.'

'No, Señor. It is at the other end. On the corner facing the pool,' Ana Maria said.

'That sounds lovely, doesn't it Ernie?'

'Better than last time when we were next to the bar and that blooming racket.'

'Here are your keys and remote for the television, Señora.'

'Gracias, Ana Maria.'

'De nada, Señora. Andrés!' said Ana Maria, turning to the young porter, 'Las maletas, por favor. Apartamento cuarenta siete.'

'Now what?' said Ernest to Florence.

'Please go with Andrés, Señor. He will take your cases to the villa. Enjoy your stay.'

The door into *La Recepción* from the road faced north. The door opposite and facing south, led to the apartments and pool area. When Ernest, holding onto his wife's arm with his left hand and holding his stick in his right, stepped into the open air and the blazing sun, he felt as though he had just put his face into an oven.

'What's your name again?' said Ernest.

'Andrés. His name's Andrés. Andrew in English, Ernie,' said Florence.

'You speak English, Andrew?' asked Ernest rather loudly.

'Si, Señor. A little,' Andrés answered modestly.

'I gather you've got the remote control for the television,' Ernest said in a slightly more normal voice.

'Si, Señor.'

'Waste of time! What would I want with television specially since it's all in Spanish.'

'No, is not all Spanish, Señor. Six English. Two German. Two Italian,' said Andrés.

'Six English? I'll tell you something, Andrew. Those six *so-called English* channels will be one English - BBC World News I'll bet you a pound to a penny. The other five will be American! Four minutes of adverts - one minute of rubbish! Complete waste of time.'

'Give over, Ernie,' said Florence. 'and mind the step!

Like all *los apartamentos* at Castillo Beach Club and probably at most of the other resorts on the island, *apartamento* 47, had thick walls, to keep the interior cool. They were painted white on the outside to reflect the sun's rays. The roof was not pitched but flat because it was cheap to build and rarely rained upon. Apartments 46 and 47 formed one unit and shared an inner dividing wall. A narrow terrace of red terracotta tiles ran across the front of the entire unit. A thick hedge of bougainvilleas divided the terrace into two and on each half stood a white plastic table and four white plastic chairs.

Andrés unlocked the glass-panelled wooden door, pulled back the curtains keeping out the sun and carried the suitcases into the bedroom. Their holiday bungalow, as Ernest called it, consisted of three rooms.

The door from the terrace – the only door in and out of the apartment – led directly into the largest room comprising the kitchen, living room, dining room (identified by the presence of a square pine table and four chairs) and spare bedroom (identified by the two-seater couch that could convert into a bed).

The second, much smaller room was the main bedroom. The third, even smaller room, was the bathroom. All the walls were white. All the floors were tiled. There were one or two framed abstract prints on the living room and bedroom walls and a mirror on the bathroom wall over the washbasin.

'Oh, this looks very nice,' said Florence.

'It's cooler in here than outside but it smells a bit musty to me, said Ernest.

'For goodness sake, Ernie!' snapped Florence. 'Cheer up! We're on holiday.'

'Where are the suitcases?' Ernest asked.

'I put them on the bed, Señor, so you not fall over them,' the porter said.

'Gracias, Andrés,' said Florence, handing the young man a tip.

'De nada, Señora. Muchas gracias, Señora! Adios Señor!' said Andrés.

'Right!' said Florence. 'I'd better go to the supermarket. I don't suppose you want to stretch your legs and come with me, Ernie?'

'No thanks. I'll stay here and unpack the cases.'

'Alright. I won't be long. Stay out of trouble,' said Florence.

'What's that supposed to mean?'

'You know *very well* what I mean, Ernie Broadbent.'

Next door, at number 46, the Walters had already settled into what Geoffrey told Janet was *nuestra casa de las vacaciones* – our holiday home. When Janet tried to call their apartment a villa,

Geoffrey patiently explained that *casa* means *house* or *home* but *villa* is Spanish for *town*.

'I've unpacked the cases, Janet. Will you be alright if I pop to *el supermercado*?'

'Yes, dear. I'll sit out here on the veranda until you get back.'

'I won't be long. I'll just get some milk and coffee. D'you fancy anything?

'A Danish pastry would be nice as long as it's fresh,' said Janet.

'Right! See you in a minute,' said Geoffrey, kissing his wife on the cheek.

'Bye!' Janet said, content to feel the sun on her slender legs.

* * * * *

Meanwhile, in the bedroom of number 47, Ernest Broadbent BSc PhD, restless as ever, was talking to himself as he tackled the suitcases that Andrés had put on the bed.

'Right! Let's see if I can get these cases unpacked before milady gets back. This must be hers. Oh, for God's sake! Why does it always weigh a ton? OK. Hangers. Where are the hangers? One, two, three, four five, six, seven, eight. There's got to be more than that. Ah, at the other side of the wardrobe. Nine, ten, eleven, twelve. O.K. That's one, two, three, four for me and one, two, three, four, five, six, seven, eight for milady. Now where's my one and only summer suit from Burtons? Ah, here it is. My God, why did I let Florrie drag me into that outfitters for this? It cost me a bomb and I had to listen to that twerp of an assistant into the bargain.'

> *'Nice fit, if I may say so, Sir. What do you think, Madam? D'you like the colour? Just feel the quality of the cloth, Sir. Lightweight. Crease-resistant. It's also stain-resistant. The perfect suit for formal and informal occasions. Would Sir like a shirt and tie to go with it? I can recommend this silk tie and Mackay 100% cotton shirt. ...'*

'Whoops! Now where's that hanger gone?'

When Geoffrey left apartment 46, he was wearing a pale beige short-sleeved shirt and white tailored shorts. His straw hat matched his shorts and his leather sandals matched his shirt. Even in his holiday attire the 6 ft 4 in tall Mr G J Walters looked every one of his inches the successful businessman. He strolled around the pool, trying to think in Spanish as he headed south for the gate leading to *Calle Virgen de la Caridad del Cobra.*

Geoffrey crossed the Virgin of the Charity of the Cobra street and ambled along in the shade. He took his time down the steep steps between *los apartementos* to *Calle San Francisco* and yet more steep steps to *Calle Virgen del Carmen* and *el supermercado.* It had been a short walk - 350 yards to be exact – from apartment 46 to the supermarket situated on the corner of Virgin of Carmen street. Geoffrey had timed his arrival to coincide with the supermarket being open at 5 p.m. after the traditional 3-hour siesta. Florence walked into el supermercado sometime later.

'Right! Let's see what I can get his nibs for supper,' thought Florence. 'Eggs still look reasonable. Mushroom omelette with chips and tomatoes. Yes. Bread rolls seem fresh. Butter. Where's the butter? Cheese. Ah! Real fruit yoghurts. Breakfast cereals. Corn Flakes and Rice Krispies. Milk? Full cream? No. Ah, 2%! Yes. *Marmelada*'s a bit steep. Oh well, we're on holiday. Strawberry jam for me. Croissants? No. I'll pop back tomorrow morning when they're in fresh. Bottle of red wine? Still cheaper here than in our local wine shop back home.'

> *'I'm sorry Mrs. Broadent. It's the Government taxes you see. They're driving us out of business. I couldn't believe it myself when I was in Majorca. The wine was so cheap there compared to here. No wonder so many Brits get drunk abroad. Not you or Dr. Broadbent of course. It's all these young soccer hooligans. We have an Amontillado on special today. '*

'What a hypocrite! The Wine Barrel go out of business with her running it? Fat chance. Whoops! I'd better get back and see how his nibs is coping with the unpacking.'

84

'Hola!' said Juanita Diaz, the maid as she approached apartment 46.

'Hello! Who are you?' said Janet

'Servicio de habitación, Señora?'

'D'you speak English?' Janet asked.

'Inglés? No. Lo siento. Necesita un rollo de papel higiénico, Señora?'

'I'm sorry. I don't understand. I do not speak Spanish,' apologised Janet.

Juanita shrugged her ample shoulders, put a spare toilet roll on the veranda table then waddled off towards number 47. She worked hard all day cleaning the apartments in readiness for the new arrivals. Checking on the supply of toilet paper and clean towels was her final task that afternoon. Her *adios*! as she left number 46 fell on deaf ears.

'I'm back, Janet. Everything alright?'

'Yes - but some woman came by and spoke to me in Spanish about something or other.'

'There's a toilet roll on the veranda table.'

'Oh!' said Janet.

'Any idea how it got there?' asked Geoffrey.

'No ... unless that woman was the cleaning lady and she put it there.'

'That's probably it. So, shall we walk down to *El Papagayo* and get some supper?'

'Lovely, Geoffrey. Give me your arm and tell me what the restaurant's called in English.'

'The Parrot. *Papagayo* is Spanish for parrot,' said Geoffrey.

Juanita Diaz was short and plump. Put less kindly but more accurately, she was fat. She had a large bosom and, as Ernest might have said, plenty to fall back on. Not surprisingly, she perspired a great deal. Put less kindly and more accurately, she was sweaty.

'Hello! That you Florrie?' said Ernest when he heard footsteps.

'Hola! Servicio de habitación, Señor,' said Juanita Diaz poking her head around the bedroom door of number 46.

'D'you speak English?' said Ernest rather loudly as usual.

'No, Señor. Lo siento. Necesita un rollo de papel higiénico, Señor?'

'No speak Spanish! No comprendez!' said Ernest just as loudly.

The journey from England to Fuerteventura was tiring enough. The walk back from the supermarket, most of the way uphill, carrying two bags of shopping made Florence even more tired. She was perspiring and feeling a trifle irritable when she entered number 46.

'What's going on?'

'Florrie? You're back,' said Ernest with relief.

'Yes, I'm back. Who's this woman. What's she doing in our bedroom with the curtains closed?' snapped Florence.

'I don't know. She just walked in. I thought it was you at first.'

'Buenas tardes, Señora. Servicio de habitación. Necesita un rollo de papel higiénico?'

'Si. Gracias,' said Florence, becoming calmer.

'Adios, Señor! ... Señora!'

'That was the maid, Ernie. She brought us a spare toilet roll.'

'Oh, the maid,' said Ernest. 'I asked her if she spoke English. All I caught was 'No, *senior* and something about *Sorrento.*'

'No, *Señor*. *Lo siento*. She was saying No, sir. Sorry!'

Florence pulled back the bedroom curtains. She was surprised that Ernest had managed to unpack and put away most of his clothes but not surprised to see that her suitcase still lay unopened on the bed.

'Here! Change into this short-sleeved shirt and shorts. I'll finish the unpacking.'

'I've put my stuff in the top drawer and I've hung my suit up,' said Ernest.

'Yes, yes! Hung it down more like. Go and sit outside. There's a chair on the veranda – on the left outside the door. I'll call you when supper's ready. Do you want your iPod?'

'Not now. I might take a nap,' said Ernest with a yawn.

'For goodness sake *be careful*. Don't put your bare feet on that black grit out there.'

'That black grit, as you call it, is *volcanic ash*. It's a mulch to keep the plant roots moist,' said Ernest who, as a non-gardener but a retired chemist, was quick to pass on his theoretical horticultural knowledge.

'All I know is it's sharp and you'll cut your feet like you did before, remember?'

'That was two years ago,' retorted Ernest. 'Two years ago!'

'The veranda's on the left outside the door,' said Florence

'I know, I know. I heard you the first time,' said Ernest.

'And don't walk into the bougainvillaea covering the screen between us and next door. You know how sharp its thorns are,' Florence snapped as her husband headed to the door.

87

* * * * *

'Are you going to stay in bed all morning?' said Florence.

'What time is it?' Ernest asked sleepily.

'It's half past eight. I've laid the table for breakfast on the veranda.'

'I didn't hear you get up,' said Ernest rubbing his hand over his bald head as though he were polishing it.

'You were out to the world. It's a wonder you didn't wake the entire resort with your snoring. I can never understand why snorers don't wake themselves up,' said Florence.

'Have they finished cleaning the pool yet?' asked Ernest.

'Yes. They finished more than half an hour ago. The pool's available from 8 am to 9 pm. You go and have your swim while I pop down to the supermarket for some croissants.'

The sun was already up but there was a breeze to move the air which was still quite cool. Florence wore sunglasses, a wide-brimmed hat, a long-sleeved blouse and white slacks to protect her fair skin. She liked walking and wore a pair of flat-heeled canvas shoes to cope with the uneven paths and roads all too common on the island. Florence left apartment number 46 for *el supermercado* just a few minutes before her neighbour left number 47.

'Janet! Where are you Janet?'

'In the bathroom, Geoffrey.'

'Everything alright?'

'Yes. I'm just putting on my bathing suit. What time is it?' asked Janet.

'Just gone half past eight,' said Geoffrey glancing at his Rolex wristwatch.

'I've done the best I can to lay the table for breakfast on the veranda.'

'So I noticed,' said Geoffrey. I'm going to fetch some croissants from *el supermercado* while you have your swim. Will you be alright?'

'Yes, of course, Geoffrey. Don't worry. I'll be fine. The pool's only outside the door.'

The supermarket on the corner of Virgin of Carmen street was certainly too small to be called *el hipermercado* and too big to be just *el mercado*. Florence collected a cart and went towards *la entrada*. The lady assistant, sitting behind the check-out at *la salida*, spoke first.

'Buenas dias, Señora. Cómo está?'

Florence smiled and responded to the *Good morning, Madam, How are you*? with, 'Muy bien y Usted?'

In response to Florence's *Very well and yourself*, the assistant smiled back and said, '*Bien, gracias!*'

Florence made a beeline for *la panaderia* to see if the croissants were fresh. Had she looked behind her she might have seen Geoffrey Walters collecting a cart and exchanging pleasantries with the attractive, dark-haired woman behind the check-out counter.

'Buenas dias, Señora. Cómo está?' said Geoffrey, politely doffing his straw hat.

'Muy bien y Usted?

'Bien, gracias. Hay croissants frescos?'

In response to his asking if the croissants were fresh, she pointed to the far left corner and replied, 'Si, Señor. Por aqui!'

The pool outside apartments 46 and 47 was narrow and oval in shape. It was connected to a larger, square-shaped pool by a small waterfall kept running continuously by a hidden circulating pump.

The water was cool bordering on cold. The water should have been kept warm by solar heating.

According to Dr Broadbent, there were at least two obvious methods. The inexpensive method was to cover the white reflecting tiles on the bottom of the pool with thick black mats that would absorb the sun's rays and heat the water. The expensive method was to install solar panels in line with the circulating pump.

'Brrrr. When are they ever going to make this a heated pool?' Ernest thought to himself as he slid off the side into the water. 'With all the sunshine they get here off the African coast, how hard can it be to install solar heating. Well at least I get the place to myself this time in the morning. Now how many strokes was it to the other end. ... Ow! D**mn it! O.K. Fifteen not sixteen. ... Oh, no. Now what?'

'Hello. Good morning. What's the water like?' said Janet as she gripped the handrails of the steps into the pool.

'Cold. Blinking cold,' said Ernest.

'Is it alright if I join you?' asked Janet.

'Why not? I'll keep to this far side if you don't mind.'

'Oh, you're right. It's not very warm, is it? I thought it was a heated pool.'

'Wouldn't that be nice. You'd think with all this sunshine it would be warmer.'

* * * * *

'Perdone, Señora.'

'Geoffrey! Geoffrey Walters!'

'Qué tal, Florence?'

'How long have you been here?'

'About five minutes,' said Geoffrey putting his hat back on his head.

'No, I mean how long have you been in Fuerteventura?'

'Flew in yesterday afternoon on Zipjet flight 197 same as you.'

'Ah, you were sitting right at the front in business class, weren't you?' said Florence.

'Yes. You walked right past me. You looked very tense,' said Geoffrey.

'I'm sorry. It's just that... Well I'm not very keen on flying.'

'Worried about taking off and landing?'

'Yes. They say that's when we're most at risk,' said Florence.

'You should read *The Polar Bear Strategy: Reflections on Risk in Modern Life* by John Ross. On second thoughts, perhaps you shouldn't.'

'Why? Why shouldn't I read it?' asked Florence.

'You've heard people say that aeroplanes are safer than cars. Well, according to John Ross that's not quite true,' said Geoffrey.

'Thank you very much. That's not what I wanted to hear,' Florence said.

'No, you should read it, Florence. You'd enjoy it. Anyway, you're not accident prone, are you?'

'No, I don't think so. Not like somebody I know,' said Florence rather sadly and thinking of her husband having his morning swim.

Unlike Geoffrey Walters, Ernest Broadbent went to a grammar school and from there to university where he studied chemistry. He gained a First Class Honours degree and after three years of research obtained his PhD. In his final year of post-graduate research he was interviewed by a scout and offered a post with Imperial Chemical

Industries. He would still be working if it had not been for the laboratory accident.

'Ouch! That's the second time I've done that,' exclaimed Janet.

'You alright? What did you do?' asked Ernest.

'I hit my hand on the edge of the pool.'

'Not looking where you were going?' asked Ernest.

'You might say that,' said Janet.

'What were you doing? Back crawl?'

'No. Just breast stroke,' said Janet.

'Got water in your eyes then I suppose,' said Ernest. 'You should wear goggles.'

'I'm afraid that wouldn't help much,' said Janet ruefully. 'Anyway, didn't I hear you shout out just now.'

'Yes. Just after you got in. I bumped my head.'

'So you weren't looking where you were going either,' said Janet.

'Actually, said Ernest, 'I thought I needed sixteen strokes for the length of the pool but it's only fifteen. ... I'm Ernie, by the way.'

'I'm Janet.'

When Florence arrived with her croissants, she found Ernest sitting on his towel on a chair on the terrace in the sunshine. His hair and his swimming trunks were still wet but the rest of him had dried in the sun.

'You'll never guess, Ernie.'

'Guess what?'

'Who I bumped into at the supermarket. Mr. Walters.'

'Who's he when he's at home,' Ernest asked.

'He's in the same evening class as me – Intermediate Spanish - at the Tech.'

'Handsome, good-looking fellow, is he?'

'Now you mention it, yes, I suppose he is in a way.'

'Anyway, how did you get on? Have a nice swim?'

'Water was cold as usual. Why they can't ...'

'Oh, don't start on again about solar heating. Go and get yourself dressed. I'll put the kettle on. Breakfast on the terrace in five minutes,' snapped Florence.

When Geoffrey arrived with his croissants, he found Janet relaxing on the couch inside the house. She had showered, dried her short dark-brown hair and changed into a short-sleeved blouse and culottes.

'Have a good swim, Janet?'

'Yes, thank you, Geoffrey. The water was a bit cold.'

'No problem getting in and out then?'

'No, none at all. I did bang my hand a couple of times but I don't think it's bruised.'

'Let's have a look,' said Geoffrey taking hold of her hand. 'You've taken a bit of skin off. I'll fetch a plaster.'

'How did you get on at the supermarket?' Janet asked.

'Fine. The croissants had just come in. They were still warm.'

'Shall I go and sit at the table on the terrace?'

'Yes, go ahead. The coffee's nearly filtered. I'll be with you in a minute,' said Geoffrey.

* * * * *

The landscape of *Fuerteventura* is a contrast of rocky coves, sandy beaches and volcanic contours, with *Pico de la Zarza* being the highest point at 2,664 ft above sea level. It is the driest of the Canary Islands, with over 3,000 hours of sunshine per year, and the closest to North Africa. There are two likely translations of the island's name. Ernest would doubtless argue the case for *strong winds*. Geoffrey preferred *good fortune*.

'Right. I've cleared the table and done the washing up. I'm going for a walk.'

'Going up that mountain to see the chipmunks, are you, Florrie?'

'Chipmunk Hill is a hill, not a mountain. Besides, it's a lovely morning and not much wind,' said Florence. 'What about you? What are you going to do?'

'Bit a weight training in the gym, perhaps,' said Ernest.

'Think you can find your way to the cave without getting lost?'

'I think so,' said Ernest. 'Anyway, I've got a tongue in my head.'

'Look!' said Florence, 'Why don't I walk you there and pick you up on the way back?'

'Yes, why not?' said Ernest, 'It'll save a lot of hassle.'

'Would you like to come for walk now, Janet?'

'No thank you, Geoffrey. I prefer the treadmill in the gym, if you don't mind.'

'Of course not. Hold my arm and I'll take you there.'

'That's nice. Then you go on your walk and collect me on your way back.'

'Sounds good. Let me know when you're ready,' said Geoffrey.

'I'm ready now if you are.'

Castillo Beach Club includes in its facilities *un gimnasio* where one can work out, take a sauna and have a massage. The Club does not mention that the gymnasium is in a windowless concrete bunker underneath the tennis court and 5-a-side soccer pitch. Once inside, Ernest had little trouble finding the multi-gym, the barbells and dumbbells. He decided to start with a pair of dumbbells.

'Ouch! Watch where you're going!' said a surprised Ernest.

'I'm sorry. Was that your foot?'

'Janet?'

'Ernie?' said a surprised Janet.

'Yes,'

'I'm trying to find the treadmill.'

'Hola! Señor! Señora!' It was the fitness instructor in charge of the gym. 'Uno momento, por favor. Voy dar las luces.'

'Do you know what he said, Ernie?' asked Janet.

'Hello Señor! Señora! I got that much ...' said Ernest.

'Inglés! Sorry. Please! A moment. I put on the lights.'

'What's your name?' asked Ernest.

'Manuel, Señor.'

'Well then, Manuel. Would you help this lady with the treadmill and then me with the multi-gym?'

'Si, Señor!'

* * * * *

'Hello, Geoffrey!'

'We meet again, Florence.'

'Where are you heading?' said Florence. 'The supermarket again?'

'No. Just out for walk,' replied Geoffrey. 'What about you?'

'A walk. Up the hill to see if any chipmunks are still there.'

'Mind if I join you?' Geoffrey asked.

'No. That would be lovely.' Said Florence.

Florence Broadbent and Geoffrey Walters met by chance attending a 20-week course in conversational Spanish run by the Workers' Educational Association for adults from all walks of life. They both came to look forward to the weekly evening class.

'So, are you staying here at the Castillo Beach Club?' Florence inquired.

'Yes, as a matter of fact we are,' said Geoffrey.

'So, we were on the same flight yesterday,' said Florence, 'and now we are in the same resort. What a strange coincidence!'

'Not strange really, Florence,' said Geoffrey with a slight smile.

'Is this your first visit?' Florence asked without noticing the odd look on his face.

'No. We came here last year. You've been here five times I believe.'

'Yes, that's right. How did you know?' said Florence with a surprised look on her face.

'Night school at the Tech. Remember? We had to talk in Spanish about our holidays.'

'So we did. I'd forgotten that. Did I tell the class we were coming here this week?'

'Yes, you did. So you see, Florence, our meeting is not entirely by chance. Shall we go and look for your chipmunks?' said Geoffrey.

When is a chipmunk not a chipmunk? When it's a striped squirrel. Chipmunks have stripes on their faces; squirrels do not. Chipmunks have cheek pouches for storing food; squirrels do not. A chipmunk runs with its tail held vertically. A squirrel runs with its tail parallel to the ground.

'There's one. Look! Over by that large rock.'

'Oh, yes, I see it now, Geoffrey. Let's sit here and see if it will come to us.'

'Why not. It'll give me a chance to take a close look at the view said Geoffrey.'

'Why are you looking at me, Mr. Walters?' said Florence. '*Caleta de Fuste* is down there. D'you know that *caleta* is Spanish for cove and *fuste* is a type of fishing boat. I've got a little book that says the horse-shoe beach is man made and the pale golden sand was imported. It must have cost a fortune.'

'D'you know you're a very attractive woman, Florence Broadbent?' said Geoffrey.

'Fuerteventura is the Canary Island closest to the North African coastline - sixty miles away,' continued Florence beginning to blush. 'It's too far over the horizon for us to see it from here even with binoculars.'

'Why should I look at the North Atlantic ocean when I can look at you?' said Geoffrey.

'Oh, look. Here he comes,' Said Florence. 'Look at that! He took that pistachio nut right out of my hand.'

'Did you know a chipmunk is a small striped squirrel (*una ardilla listada*)?'

'No, I didn't know that,' said Florence. 'I know *ardilla* is Spanish for squirrel.'

'If it hasn't got stripes on its face then it's not a chipmunk.'

'So I just gave a nut to…'

'A ground squirrel (*una ardilla moruna*),' said Geoffrey, gazing into her eyes.

'Look at the time,' exclaimed Florence. 'I'd better be getting back. Ernie will be wondering where I am.'

* * * * *

'Señor! Señora! Please. I close the gym now,' said Manuel.

'What's the time?' Ernest asked.

'12 o'clock, Señor!'

'How do I switch off this treadmill?' Janet asked.

'I will do it, Señora!' said Manuel. 'Please, I help you with your jacket.'

'Thank you, Manuel,' said Janet.

'De nada, Señora.'

'D'you mind if I take your arm, Ernie?' said Janet.

'Well, no, O.K. Actually I was going to ask you...'

'Señor! This cane is yours, no?' said Manuel.

'What? Oh, yes. Thank you,' said Ernest.

98

'Please. I hold the door open for you,' said Manuel. 'Adios!'

'Thank you. Crikey! It's hot outside.'

'Hmm, yes. I love to feel the sun on my face,' said Janet squeezing Ernest's arm.

'So where's your apartment, Janet?'

'It's by the pool, Ernie.'

'And mine. O.K. If we keep to this path we should get there.'

Manuel closed and locked the door of *el gymnasio* and watched admiringly as Ernest and Janet made their way up the path.

'Oh, dear. The gym's closed,' exclaimed Florence. 'I told Ernie I'd meet him here on my way back from my walk. I hope he's alright.'

'Why shouldn't he be?' said Geoffrey.

'You don't know my Ernie,' said Florence wryly.

'He probably gave up waiting and has gone back to your apartment. Where is your apartment exactly?'

'We're right by the swimming pool,' said Florence.

'So are we,' Said Geoffrey. 'Actually I was supposed to collect Janet from the gym. Perhaps she's gone back with your husband.'

'That'll be it. Yes, I'll bet that's what's happened,' said Florence. 'What a relief.'

'How about that?' said Geoffrey. 'My wife's with your husband and I'm here with you.'

'Geoffrey Walters! Were you flirting with me back there on Chipmunk Hill. Because if you were, you can stop. Stop right now,' said Florence. 'My Ernie can be a bit of a trial at times - especially since his accident - but he's my husband and I married him for better, for worse.'

'I apologise, Florence. I suppose I was being a bit of a flirt,' confessed Geoffrey, 'but you do know you are a very attractive woman. Will you forgive me?'

'I'm flattered,' said Florence. 'Of course I forgive you.'

'Friends?' said Geoffrey with a broad smile.

'*Amigos*!' said Florence. 'No more flirting. Agreed?'

'Agreed, mi amiga!' said Geoffrey.

'Alright then. Let's go and find our spouses.'

'You said Ernie had an accident...'

'Yes, it was a chemical leak from a fume cupboard in the lab where he was working.'

'What happened? Was it serious?' Geoffrey asked with genuine concern.

'Yes and no. He was lucky in one way, you know,' said Florence. 'He wasn't burned or scarred but the chemical he was working on was a neurological toxin. It affected his eyes.'

'What do you mean *affected his eyes*?' said Geoffrey uneasily.

'Ernie's blind.'

'Oh my God! He's blind?'

'Yes!' said Florence. 'Didn't I tell you?'

'No!' said Geoffrey. 'This is terrible. We've got to hurry.'

'Why? What's the problem? Your Janet's safe with him.'

'You don't understand. It's the blind leading the blind,' said Geoffrey.

'Your Janet's blind? She's blind too? Good gracious.'

* * * * *

'Well, Ernie, we've found the swimming pool. No doubt about that.'

'We certainly did, Janet, we certainly did. No doubt at all.'

* * * * *

Epilogue

In October 2005, following new Government rules, Thomas Cook Airlines allowed one blind person, travelling from Gatwick to the Canaries, to purchase an extra seat for their guide dog in the main cabin. The limit was just one dog with one blind person per flight. So one or other of my fictitious characters, Ernie or Janet, might have taken their guide dog on holiday if I had given them one and if I had endowed them with the patience to deal with all the rules and regulations of micro-chipping, anti-rabies vaccinations and EU Pet Passports.

Fuerteventura is popular with visitors wanting to avoid the more commercial tourism of Gran Canaria, Lanzarote and Tenerife. Aside from the resorts, the only man-made attractions are La Lajita Zoo and Baku Water Park. The Barbary ground squirrel was introduced to Fuerteventura in 1965 and became a pest, with numbers estimated at more than 300,000. Like the chipmunk, the squirrel is a rodent. For the sake of the tourist trade, these ground squirrels in Fuerteventura are, erroneously, called chipmunks!

The expression Where there's muck there's brass *– meaning that there is money to be made doing dirty, unattractive work - originated in Yorkshire, England in the 20th century. Brass is still slang for money and derives from the copper and bronze coins issued as long ago as the 17th century.*

The Workers' Educational Association (WEA) is the largest voluntary provider of adult education in the United Kingdom. Founded in 1903, it is now one of the biggest charities operating at regional and national level with over 450 local branches. The WEA runs over 10,000 courses, for relatively small tuition fees, each year for more than 110,000 adults.

* * * * *

Keep reading for an excerpt from the first story in Volume 4 of
Michael C. Cox's collection of short stories

Facts and Fantasies

available from Amazon as an individual volume or part of the

Omnibus Collection of Short Stories

in paperback and electronic book form

* * * * *

THE APPLE CART

The small retailer has not yet been entirely driven to the wall by the supermarket chain. Some have survived as street traders in open markets which have become popular tourist attractions, e.g. Petticoat Lane in London and Albert Cuypstraat in Amsterdam. In our house here in Canada we still have knick-knacks from flea markets as far afield as the Canary Islands, France and Mexico. This story was conceived as a small tribute to the many stall owners we have encountered around the world. As my research and writing of it proceeded, this story became more importantly a tribute to my Canadian friends and SEARIC - their charitable Society for the Education and Assistance of Rural Indian Children.

* * * * *

The day began like any other Friday. Kavi Cheema switched off the alarm just before it could go off at 3 a.m. In front of the wall mirror above the hand washbasin in his bedroom he carefully trimmed his already close-cropped beard before he showered in the tiny cubicle in the corner. In the kitchen he had a breakfast of orange juice and Muesli (a breakfast cereal of wheat flakes, toasted oats, fruit and nuts) over which he poured some milk.

In the hallway he pulled on his overalls, tied his shoe-laces and put on his woollen hat and gloves. In his father's old Ford minivan he checked the shopping list on his clip-board, started the engine, checked the blind spot over his right shoulder and moved off. Kavi was a proud member of the Institute of Advanced Motorists and strove to maintain its high standards of driving. He arrived safely at 'London's Larder' just after 4 a.m. without breaking any speed limits or contravening any road traffic acts.

New Covent Garden Market, set up in 1961 on the site of the old locomotive works at Nine Elms, is the wholesale food & flower market controlled by the government. Kavi collected what his father would have needed from the companies he had dealt with regularly. As always, just like his father did, he left the apples until last. As always, he took his time to inspect each individual apple. He had become immune to the supplier's banter about his father's minivan.

'Old 'enry Ford made it 'ere then, Kev!' In the market everybody called him Kevin or Kev – never Kavi.

'Nah,' replied Kavi, mimicking their London Cockney accents, 'Ee packed up at Battersea an' I 'ad ter shove 'im the rest of the way 'ere, cor blimey.'

Kavi gave time for the laughter to die down then headed for Old 'enry Ford.

He was back in Southall and able to unload the van at his father's stall in The Broadway before 6 a.m. If the traffic warden caught him unloading after 6 a.m., when restrictions applied, he'd face a parking fine – known in law as a fixed penalty or penalty charge. Kavi knew it was not a criminal matter but in his position he could not afford even to break a local authority traffic regulation.

It was just after half past six when he parked Old 'enry Ford outside his parents' terraced house in Oswald Road and put the resident's permit on the dashboard. When he opened the front door Kavi heard the Panjabi radio broadcast coming from the kitchen. His mother was up. She was probably getting breakfast ready for Rajender, his 11 year old son who was just coming down the stairs. He was in his pyjamas.

Raj had been woken up by the noise of the minivan pulling up outside the house. Kavi still could not get used to the rattle of the engine and the squealing brakes. 'The BMW 5 series saloon, or any BMW car for that matter, would never make this noise,' he thought, as he slammed the driver's door three times before it finally shut.

'Kavi sat sree akaal,' said Mrs. Cheema as she poured glasses of orange juice for her son and grandson.

'Ma sat sree akaal,' he replied in Panjabi to his mother before saying in English to his son 'Good morning, Raj.'

'Hi, Dad,' his son replied in English with the slightest hint of a French accent.

'When is your maths test today?'

'First thing this morning.'

'Good luck. Come to the stall after school. You can give me a hand and tell me how you got on. OK?'

'OK, Dad,'

'Here's an apple for your teacher but don't give it to her until you've got your test result. I don't want to defend you against bribery and corruption charges.'

Kavi walked up Oswald Road to The Broadway to prepare the family stall for business just as his father used to do. 'Display all our fruit and vegetables so our customers can see what they are buying,' his father would say. Kavi did just that. He took extra care with the apples. Each one was individually polished before being arranged into a tall pyramid on a little wooden handcart at the front of the stall.

The cart belonged to Kavi's father who used it to sell fruit and vegetables door to door when he first came to England. When they opened their business in the Broadway, his father named the stall 'The Apple Cart' and kept his little handcart at the front as a reminder of their humble beginnings.

'Everything must be tip top and fair price,' his father insisted. 'Always be friendly and polite so the customers will be coming back again and again.' When Kavi's father died, many of his customers came to pay their respects and offer their condolences. Kavi often recalled his father's story about a Brahmin, who had an infinite supply of something that was absolutely worthless until he gave it away.

'What was it that the Brahmin had?' Kavi's father would ask. When Kavi pretended he didn't know, his father would smile and say, 'Kavi, the Brahmin had what I am just giving to you. You are receiving smile. Remember, Kavi, to be giving everybody smiles.'

* * * * *

When Kavi opened the stall at 7:30 a.m. he smiled at his first customer. As he was serving her, a small group of pupils from Beaconsfield School sauntered up and stood close to the apple cart. He was handing the lady her change when the group turned and ran as the pyramid started to collapse. Apples were falling off the cart and bouncing in every direction.

It happened so quickly. One minute there was a pyramid of polished apples. A moment later much of the fruit was lying bruised or broken on the floor. The worst of it was that Kavi saw his son, Raj, in the group running down the road. And he had an apple in his hand.

That Friday afternoon Kavi closed the stall early and at 3 o'clock marched down Oswald Street to Beaconsfield School. He was standing in the foyer when the bell signalled the end of school. 'There's yer dad by the door,' said Adil, 'and 'e don't look 'appy.' As soon as he saw him, Raj guessed his father was all out of smiles.

'Hi Dad!'

'Who are these boys?' asked Kavi.

'Adil, Sunil and Vijay. They're my friends.'

'Which one of you upset my apples this morning?' asked Kavi, glaring at the three boys.

Kavi hadn't actually seen Raj take the apple from the cart but he had seen him running away with an apple in his hand.

'Circumstantial evidence - two or more facts taken together to infer a conclusion about something unknown,' Kavi reminded himself.

'They didn't do it, Dad. I did. It was an accident.'

'What do you mean, it was an accident?'

'We dared 'im.' said Adil. 'We told 'im 'e 'ad to pinch an apple if 'e wanted to be in our gang. Vijay told 'im which one to pinch.'

'Vijay told 'im to grab the corner apple at the bottom. We didn't fink them apples would fall off the cart,' lied Sunil.

'We are very sorry, Mr. Cheema,' said Vijay.

'You don't look sorry, any of you.' said Kavi. 'Take those silly grins off your faces.'

'I'm sorry, Dad. I didn't think.'

'That's your trouble,' said Kavi, 'you don't always think. Those apples will come out of your pocket money. Let's go home.'

At that moment, Raj's class teacher appeared. 'Good afternoon Miss Kumar,' the boys chorused.

'Good afternoon Raj, Adil, Sunil, Vijay,' she said, smiling back at them. The attractive, dark-haired young teacher then looked at Kavi. 'Good afternoon! Mr. Cheema, is it?'

'Yes. Kavi Cheema. Good afternoon Miss Kumar,' he said, giving her his broadest smile.

'Will you be coming to the parents' evening next week?'

'Ah, yes, the parents' evening. Next week. I think so. Goodness me. Yes. Yes.'

'Good!' she said, 'It's our first meeting of the school year and the first chance for me to meet the parents of my pupils. I look forward to seeing you there, Mr. Cheema.' She smiled, this time at Kavi, and headed for the staff room.

Raj saw his dad's smile vanish as soon as Miss Kumar was out of sight. First the apples. Now he was in trouble for losing his teacher's letter about parents' evening. To make matters worse, he didn't think he had done his best in the maths test that morning.

As they walked home side by side, Kavi recalled how it had been when he misbehaved and let his father down. He remembered how his father forgave him especially when he owned up right away and didn't try to put the blame on somebody else. 'Kavi,' he would say, 'you are being foolish boy but I forgive you because you owned up and were sorry.'

'Rajender!'

'Yes Dad!'

'Why didn't I know there was a parents' evening next week?'

'It's my fault, Dad. I forgot to bring home the letter. I'm sorry. I just forgot.'

'I felt foolish when your teacher asked me if I was coming.'

'Sorry, Dad.'

'Well, alright. I forgive you. Don't forget again.'

'No, Dad.'

'Now about those apples... '

'Yes, Dad.'

'If I tell you how many were ruined, how much each apple cost me and how much a customer would have paid me for one, can you work out how many weeks it will take you to repay me if I deduct half your weekly pocket money?'

'Yes, Dad.'

FACTS AND FANTASIES – Volume 1

1. The lawn

This story is a fiction based upon facts personally reported to me and upon events I experienced firsthand. For instance, I knew a chemist, who left a major chemical company, solved a pollution problem, published a book of walks to unusual places, brewed his own wine and who, inspired by the fall of a cast iron gutter that might have killed his son, made his fortune in PVC guttering and downpipes.

2. The Axeman cometh

On the 12th of December 1966, Frank Mitchell absconded from Her Majesty's prison high on Dartmoor in the English county of Devon. The following story is true and as accurate as my memory permits. I have not changed the names of the people involved, so I apologise in advance to those (living or dead) mentioned herein who might feel that I have portrayed them in a worse light than I portrayed myself.

3. A tick in a Box

A Canadian source defines bureaucracy as a hierarchy of authority and a system of rules, regulations and record keeping characterized by division of labour and specialization of functions. A British source defines bureaucracy as an excessively complicated administrative procedure. After reading this story, the reader will, I trust, take more care than I did when completing any official form but heed the words of Robert Frost, "If we couldn't laugh, we would all go insane."

4. The journey of a canvas bag

Air is a liquid at minus 200 degrees centigrade. In their research at Bristol University, chemistry students often needed liquid air for their experiments. They kept the liquid in open-necked vacuum flasks to slow its evaporation. This story is based upon an incident that actually took place on a train travelling from Bristol to Southampton around 1958-59. Apart from Bob, all the characters are figments of my imagination. Two of the characters appear in the first story in volume 2 of my collected short stories.

* * * * *

FACTS AND FANTASIES – Volume 2

1. The best laid schemes

My parents, like many people after World War II, did not have a car. I was fortunate. John, a friend of mine, taught me to drive his small Morris Oxford which he used for work. He was a travelling door-to-door brush salesman. John liked some of the people he met but disliked the job, so he eventually went back to work for an insurance company. He disliked that work rather less but some of his co-workers rather more. The idea for this story stems from my recollection of John's account of life as a salesman and an insurance clerk.

2. What are the chances?

Certain people and chance events change our lives. They make us reconsider our beliefs, discard our old habits and gain a new sense of purpose and direction. This true story is about my father and an event that achieved quite the opposite. It gives credence to the adage 'Old habits die hard' and, dare I say it, to the adage 'You can't teach an old dog new tricks.' In regard to the first, I fear that I follow in my father's footsteps.

3. A mixed blessing

This story is a confession of a crime I committed out of false pride and in a moment of weakness more than forty years ago. By now both the statute of limitations and the statute of repose have probably run out and the long arm of the law in England is unlikely to reach across the Atlantic Ocean to Canada but, to be on the safe side, I ask you to believe the name of my victim and the associated geographical details to be pure fiction.

4. The lawnmower

This is a true story. By that I mean I have described a real incident to the best of my ability and memory. However, I have not disclosed the names of the real people involved. Any former friends and neighbours who think they recognise themselves and take exception to being excluded or included will, I trust, accept my apologies and neither strike me from their Christmas card list nor add me to their to-be-sued list.

FACTS AND FANTASIES – Volume 4

1. The apple cart

The small retailer has not yet been entirely driven to the wall by the supermarket chain. Some have survived as street traders in open markets which have become popular tourist attractions, e.g. Petticoat Lane in London and Albert Cuypstraat in Amsterdam. In our house here in Canada we still have knick-knacks from flea markets as far afield as the Canary Islands, France and Mexico. This story was conceived as a small tribute to stall owners we encountered around the world. As my research and writing proceeded, it became a tribute to my Canadian friends and SEARIC - their charitable Society for the Education and Assistance of Rural Indian Children.

2. Across a crowded room

On the 6th of August 2010, on the cruise liner Celebrity Constellation, Maureen and I celebrated our Golden Wedding Anniversary. This is the story of how I met my wife. Some of my scientific friends suggest we travel through life encountering people haphazardly as particles collide according to Einstein's mathematical theory of random walk. Maureen and I met by chance they say. Some of my non-scientific friends suggest otherwise. It was kismet they say. Whatever the case, of one thing I can be absolutely sure, I am glad we met.

3. The disappearing chemistry teacher

The central incident in this story occurred in 1960 during my first year of full-time teaching and is described as accurately as my memory will allow. I have given fictitious names to the school and the people involved just in case the long arm of the law could stretch 50 years back in time and instigate prosecutions under the 1974 Health and Safety at Work Act.

4. An alarming business

This story is set in Broadstone, Dorset, where I lived and worked from the Easter of 1971 until I moved to Canada in December 2000. The characters and their goings-on are figments of my imagination but inspired by certain events in which I was involved and by some people whom I held in high regard and about whom I should not, nay would not intentionally write a libellous word.